Property Of
ADULT EDUCATION
NORTHWEST COMMUNITY COLLEGE

-2000-02

D0959570

THE

BUCKLE

Property Of
ADULT EDUCATION DEPT.
NORTHWEST COMMUNITY COLLEGE

NOVELS FOR ADULT LEARNERS

THE
BUCKLE

DON SAWYER

CENTRE FOR CURRICULUM, TRANSFER AND TECHNOLOGY

VICTORIA, BRITISH COLUMBIA

THE BUCKLE
by Don Sawyer
Copyright © 1997 by the Province of British Columbia
Ministry of Education, Skills and Training
All rights reserved.

This novel has been written especially for adults learners improving their reading skills.
The development and production was funded by the Province of British Columbia,
Ministry of Education, Skills and Training.

Project coordination: Centre for Curriculum, Transfer and Technology
Design and production coordination: Bendall Books
Cover design and illustration: Bernadette Boyle

CANADIAN CATALOGUING IN PUBLICATION DATA

Sawyer, Don.
    The buckle
    (Novels for adult learners)
    ISBN 0-7718-9493-7
    1. High interest-low vocabulary books. 2. Readers
(Adult) I. Centre for Curriculum, Transfer and
Technology. II. Title. III. Series.
PS8587.A3B82 1997   428'.62   C97-960067-7
PR9199.3S3B82 1997

ORDER COPIES FROM

Marketing Department
Open Learning Agency
4355 Mathissi Place
Burnaby, BC, Canada V5G 4S8
Telephone: 604-431-3210
Toll-free: 1-800-663-1653
Fax: 604-431-3381
Order Number: VA0190

CONTACT FOR INFORMATION

Centre for Curriculum, Transfer and
Technology
5th Floor, 1483 Douglas Street
Victoria, BC, Canada V8W 3K4
Telephone: 250-387-6065
Fax: 250-387-9142

ALSO IN THE SERIES, NOVELS FOR ADULT LEARNERS

CROCODILES AND RIVERS by Don Sawyer
FROZEN TEARS by Don Sawyer
THE MAILBOX by Kate Ferris
THE SCOWLING FROG by Kate Ferris
THREE WISE MEN by Kate Ferris

ACKNOWLEDGEMENTS

While this is a work of fiction, the author is deeply indebted to Mick Gabert for sharing his experiences and contributing significantly to the writing of this book.

1

Luke walked slowly through the crowd. Most people at the rodeo were wearing jeans, cowboy boots and cowboy hats, just like he was. But there was something different about Luke. His jeans were worn white in the thighs. His hat was stained with sweat, and the boots he wore weren't shiny and made out of ostrich skin. They were black, creased and scuffed at the toe. And there was something grim about the thin line of his lips. Or maybe it was the two dark eyes that were hard and shiny like polished stones.

A young woman in a frilled, purple satin shirt walked by. "Hey, Luke."

Luke looked up and managed a short smile, revealing the gap where his bottom two teeth should have been. "Hey, honey." He didn't know her. She was just another rodeo groupie. But right now he wasn't thinking about women. He was thinking about the bull he had drawn for that afternoon's ride. Sundial.

When the bulls had been posted that morning, there had been a small huddle of cowboys staring intently at the list.

He had suddenly felt a hand wallop him on the back. He'd spun around, his fist cocked, and had stared into Harvey Machele's wide grin. "Hey, slow down there little Luke." Harvey had crossed his hands in front of his face, pretending to protect himself. "For a little guy you sure are quick to duke it out."

Luke had felt the tension seep out of him, and had managed a tight smile. "Sorry, Harvey. If I'd known it was only you I would have just kicked you in the nuts."

"That's what I like about you, Luke. You're just one nice guy." Harvey had pointed up at the list with his chin. "But hey, you got more than me to worry about. Drawing Sundial for your second ride. It's kind of make or break, isn't it?"

Luke had resumed staring silently at the list as if he could make it change if he glared hard enough. "Yeah. Never been ridden. Toughest bull on the circuit."

"You don't have to tell me," Harvey said. "I rode him in Cranbrook." He gave a short laugh. "Or I should say I *tried* to ride him in Cranbrook."

Luke's dark eyes flickered up at the taller man. "Yeah? What was he like?"

"Oh, kind of like riding a case of detonated dynamite. He went off so fast and in so many directions I hardly had a chance to get seated. I can't tell you much about his bucking pattern. Explosion is pretty close." Harvey gave another short laugh. "It was a relief to hit the dirt.

"Of course, you can look on the bright side, too," Harvey continued.

"Yeah, what's that?" muttered Luke.

"If you ride him, you'll get one hell of a score. And $3,000 on top of your prize money." At this rodeo, a cowboy who rode a bull never ridden before got $3,000. But of course there was a reason Sundial hadn't been ridden. The rumour was the big Brahman was unrideable, and both men knew it. "But hey, you're a short little wiry guy. You've got the build to do it."

"Yeah, maybe," Luke agreed halfheartedly. "I'll see you over at the chutes, eh?"

"You bet. I may be out of the money, but I'll handle your flank strap." Harvey had been thrown on his first ride the day before so he was eliminated from the second round. "You're going in fourth," he added seriously. "You pull this one off and you'll take first or second."

From the posting, Luke had gone to his truck parked in the dusty lot behind the rodeo grounds. He had climbed into the camper on the back. It was old and smelled like dirty clothes and sweat inside. The small table was jammed with used glasses. He had opened a cupboard and pulled out a half-empty bottle of 5-Star rye, sloshed some into one of the glasses and sat down heavily on the bed. He drank the rest of the bottle in 15 minutes.

That had been a few hours ago. Now, slightly drunk, he made his way through the spectators toward the announcer's stand where the bulls were posted. He checked the list again, just to make sure. Nothing had changed. His name was still beside bull 47. Sundial. Then he glanced over at the glass case next to the bulletin board. In it were several trophies and a couple of silver buckles with bucking horses and bulls on them. But in the middle, in a box lined with red velvet, was the one thing Luke wanted more than anything else in the world.

The BC Provincial Championship buckle was about 12 inches in diameter. Along the outside edge of its shiny silver surface it was laced with gold. Six red garnets were set just inside the lacing in a circle. Inside this a gold bull with a cowboy on his back reared three inches high. A gold scroll across the top read "BC Championships: Bull Riding." Underneath was another scroll. It was blank. The name of the year's champion would be engraved there. It was the most beautiful buckle Luke had ever seen. He was ranked sixth in the province. If he kept riding well, and stayed out of the hospital, he could get it. The provincials were just a month away in Kamloops. He could get it. But Sundial, all 2,000 pounds of him, stood in the way. If he could ride Sundial, he could ride any bull in the province. He would have the respect he'd never quite managed in his four years of riding. The respect he deserved but had never received.

He thought back bitterly to his first introduction to rodeoing. That had been at the juvenile camp. He'd pulled 12 break and enters before they caught him climbing out of the window of an insurance office. He'd gotten six months for that. The camp had been up near Barriere, north of Kamloops, a kind of ranch with guards. They'd done chores, learned to handle the animals. And they had learned to ride. He was pretty good with the horses, both bareback and saddle broncs. But it was the bulls he had loved. He had never felt such power before. He was 150 pounds sitting on 2,000 pounds of bull. And he was in control. He was on top.

After one ride he jumped down from the bull, which was still bucking and kicking in the ring. His eyes were shining and he walked over to the fence by the instructor. The instructor had been a champion bull rider 30 years before. His face was dark, lined by the sun and dust. He had looked at Luke. A smile played around his lips.

"Nothing quite like it, eh?"

Luke looked up. "What's that?"

The older man glanced at the bull, still kicking. "Bulls have four times the power of a horse. If you want a feeling of power, get on a bull. The rush. The adrenaline. There's no drug like it. I know. I tried them all."

"Yeah," Luke said. "I like the power."

"You're good at it," the instructor said. "Don't get too arrogant, too cocky, and you could be champion some day."

That seemed like a long time ago. He looked back at the buckle in the case. Sundial.

2

The big Brahman bull stood restlessly in the chute. They're the deadliest, Luke thought. The nastiest. The trickiest. The hump behind the bull's massive head wobbled slightly as he snorted and shuffled between the boards. They can do so many things. They twist. They spin. And they love to dance all over you. They'll kill you if they get a chance.

"Mean-looking, eh?" Harvey stood beside Luke staring at the huge silver-grey bull in front of them.

"Not as mean as me," Luke said.

"OK, cowboy," an official yelled. "Up on the bull."

Suddenly the bull reared up against the front gate, bellowing. His front hooves clattered against the metal pipe of the gate. The gate man jumped back in alarm. "Man, you ride this guy," Harvey muttered, "and you could get a hundred."

Luke said nothing. One hundred points was the highest score a rider could earn. He'd never seen it happen. The best he'd ever gotten was a 94.

Luke pulled a leather glove on his right hand. "Let's go," he said.

"And Harvey, when you pull the flank strap, don't make it too tight." As the rider came out of the chute, the cinch man pulled a leather belt in front of the bull's rear legs. If it was too tight the bull became "cinch bound" and wouldn't buck. "I'm too pumped for a stroll across the arena."

"Ha," Harvey replied. "You should be so lucky."

Luke climbed slowly over the boards, making sure he stayed out of sight of the bull moving uneasily inside the chute. Luke knew that if Sundial caught a glimpse of him he could start rearing again. Luke eyed the horns slicing through the dusty air. He'd seen other riders get gored and trampled before even getting out of the chute.

He straddled the bull, his feet on each side of the chute, and slowly lowered himself down onto the bull's back just behind his hump. Harvey helped Luke get the rigging around the bull's neck and handed it up to him. It was a braided leather rope, and the bell attached to the bottom clanged uneasily as the bull shuffled under his weight. Luke worked the resin into the palm of his glove until it was warm and sticky. Then he rubbed the resin into the rope until it was tacky. He put his hand through the handle braided into the rigging and cinched up the rope as tight as he could get it. He felt the bull shudder nervously as his hand sank into the animal's back. Then he began to wrap the rigging around his hand.

Luke hesitated as he brought the rope across his palm and around the back of his hand. Should he use a suicide wrap? The usual wrap pulled loose when the rider was either thrown or jumped off the bull. The suicide wrap—a half hitch around the thumb—kept him bound to the bull until he untied the rope. It could give a rider an edge. It held him a little firmer, kept him on a little longer. But it was dangerous too. Luke had seen cowboys rip their thumbs off when thrown. And if they couldn't get loose, they could be smashed against the boards. The last time Luke had tried it he had broken two ribs.

He shook his head slightly and brought the rope back around his palm and yanked it tight. This bull was too dangerous. He'd go with the regular wrap.

Luke sat back slowly, making sure his spurs never touched the bull. If the big Brahman had felt those spurs, he could have dumped Luke right in the chute and trampled him with no place to escape. Luke was almost sitting on top of his right hand cinched into Sundial's back. Luke wanted to be sure that he was planted firmly. He wanted to be glued to the bull when the gate opened.

He pulled up on the rigging so all his strength was in his arm. He felt the rigging tighten up. The rope was like an electrical cord carrying the power of the bull up through his taut arm. He felt the exhilaration again—over 2,000 pounds of bull shifted uneasily underneath him. And he was in control.

Luke set his feet with the toes pointed in at the bull's shoulders and sat straight up. Half the points was dependent on the animal. The other half was on his performance. He didn't want to get marked down for bad form. Not this time. Too much was riding on this bull.

"Eight seconds!" He heard Harvey yell from behind him. "Just eight seconds and you've got one hell of a payday!"

"Chute!" Luke screamed. The gateman standing in the arena yanked on the rope and the gate flew open.

As Luke expected, Sundial leapt out into the arena like a dart. Everything was oddly quiet now, and slow. It was as if someone had put a movie on slow motion and turned off the sound. Luke kept his head up, but his eyes were locked onto the bull's shoulders. This would tell him which way the animal was going next. If his shoulders dipped, he was going to dive. If both rippled and twisted, he was going straight up. If his left shoulder dropped, he was going into a left spin.

Luke was vaguely aware of his left hand grabbing a handful of hair. He had done this for so long it was almost unconscious. It kept his left hand out of the way and off the animal. If it touched the bull, his ride was over.

The bull suddenly dove right and went into a spin. Luke dug his spur into Sundial's left shoulder to straighten him up. He didn't want to let the powerful bull create a "well"—a spin so powerful it sucks the rider into the dirt like a hurricane.

Sundial lunged up to his left, and Luke wondered how many seconds had gone by. On the back of a bull, eight seconds felt like an eternity. He could see the people spinning in the stands. He could see the clown flash by, waving his hands. He even noticed the judges looking intently at him from the judging stand. It all flew by in slow motion. Surely eight seconds were up. Then Sundial's shoulders rippled.

The fierceness of the explosion caught Luke by surprise. He'd never had a bull lunge upward, almost like a bronc, so high, so powerfully, twisting all the time. Sundial had had enough. Suddenly Luke was in the air. Then he hit the dirt.

Now there was sound again. The yelling of the crowd. The hollering of the clown. The pounding hoofs of Sundial, who had spun around and was headed for him. Luke jumped to his feet. He dodged out of the way as the huge Brahman charged by him. Trying to get his breath, he ran to the fence. Hands helped him over the boards.

"Good try, Luke," one of the old cowboys said to him. "You only missed by a few seconds."

Luke was still leaning against the rails wondering if he'd broken his ribs again when Harvey ran up.

"You all right?"

"Lost my entry fee. Broke a few ribs. Missed a chance at over 3,000 bucks. Couldn't be better. But thanks for asking."

Harvey grinned. "Man, I thought you had it. And then he shot up like a rocket. Just took off. He must have had his front feet 10 feet off the ground."

"I'm glad I was able to be so entertaining," Luke grunted, feeling his side gingerly.

Harvey helped Luke back to the riders' area and into one of two old lawn chairs near Harvey's pick up. In the background they heard the crowd yell as another rider came out of the chute.

Harvey pulled two bottles of Labatt's Blue out of a beat-up cooler between the lawn chairs. He twisted the cap off one and gave it to Luke. Then he opened the other and sat down heavily in the second chair.

"So, you headed up to Williams Lake next week?" Harvey asked.

"What's the entry fee?"

"Two-fifty an event. But the prize money is good. And you could use the points for the championship."

Luke tipped his bottle and sucked down the beer. "I was counting on at least getting my entry money back today."

"Yeah, me too. But at least I've got a job."

Luke sneered. "You call pumping gas a job?"

Harvey just grinned. "Well, it makes my entry money. What about you? You going?"

"I'll be there."

Harvey finished his beer and fished another out of the cooler. "How are you going to get the money?"

Luke was quiet for a minute. "I'll get it," he said finally.

3

It was dark and raining as Luke drove into Vernon. He had grown up in Enderby, some 45 kilometres up the Okanagan Valley. But he had gotten into too much trouble there. He couldn't drive around town without the cops following him. And why not? Wherever Luke was, something bad was likely to happen.

So now he lived in Vernon. He had a small apartment in an old building on the north side of town. It was basically a single room with a bathroom and a tiny bedroom. Not much bigger than some cells Luke had been in. But Luke didn't have much, didn't need much. And he didn't stay around much.

Luke grabbed his bag out of the back of the truck and walked up the stairs to his floor. In front of his door he fumbled with the keys. Finally he found the right one and let himself in the door. He didn't like standing out in the hall too long. He didn't know any of his neighbours, and he didn't want to. The last thing he wanted was for some grinning fool come up and introduce himself.

He got the light on and threw his bag on the old brown chesterfield. He made himself a peanut butter sandwich at the small counter between the stove and the sink. He took a beer out of the refrigerator and twisted the top off. He flicked on the TV and sat down on the recliner. Stuffing was oozing out of holes in the arms, and there was a long crack in the worn seat. Luke stared blankly at the screen.

It was going to cost him $250 for the entry fee at Williams Lake, even if he only rode the bulls. And then there were meals and gas. He needed $500. Ha. That was about all he got from welfare for an entire month.

Luke had tried working. Construction mainly. And he was pretty good at it. If he'd learned one thing from his father's beatings it was how to work hard. But he couldn't stand anyone telling him what to do. As soon as a boss ordered him around too much or used the wrong tone, Luke was out of there. Or if another worker looked at him the wrong way, said the wrong thing, Luke would backhand him. How many jobs had ended in fights? So Luke developed quite a reputation as a scrapper. And as trouble.

Since he'd walked away from the alcoholism and beatings of his home at 13, Luke had been on his own. He'd learned to live by his wits. But not always within the law. At first it had just been break and enters. Then he moved up to armed robberies. He'd done some time, but generally he'd been pretty smart.

Luke finished his beer and walked into his bedroom. He took a locked box from a shelf and opened it with a key. Inside a .45 pistol gleamed dully. He took the revolver and put it on the bed. Then he took out the box of shells and loaded the gun.

He had been around guns almost since his first robbery. They were easy to get. His uncles, who were in and out of jail all the time, told him whom to see. He liked .38's because they were smaller. But they didn't scare people as much as the .45. And the huge magnums were too big and cumbersome. He settled on .45's.

He grabbed a garbage bag from another corner of the closet. He reached in and pulled out three or four Halloween masks. He tossed them on the bed. He looked at the Dracula and werewolf masks, but grinned when he saw the Porky Pig mask. He felt kind of playful tonight.

He shoved the gun into his jacket pocket and stuffed the mask inside his coat. He took a blue cloth bag from a drawer and put that in his other pocket. Then he slipped a pair of black leather gloves on and left the apartment.

The Chevron station sat back off the highway. Luke stood in the shadows between the station and a closed Kentucky Fried Chicken restaurant. He watched for several minutes. No customers drove up. The single attendant was sitting at the counter reading a paperback and sipping a can of Diet Coke. He was young—not more than 20. He would scare easily. Luke slipped the mask over his face. He felt the adrenaline pump through him. Almost like getting on a bull, he thought. Almost as good, but not quite. Staying in the shadows, he walked quickly around the garage and pushed open the door to the station.

The attendant looked up as the door opened, and his eyes showed confusion. Before he had a chance to react, Luke pulled the .45 out of his pocket and placed it on the counter. His right hand was over the gun. The barrel was pointing at the attendant.

Luke always kind of liked this part. He saw the colour change in the attendant's face. The blood drained from the roots of his brown hair. He was grey-white, the colour of putty. His eyes were wide and dancing with fear. He dropped his book and it shut slowly on the counter. The boy's hands instinctively went up and he jerked back from the counter, knocking over the stool he had been sitting on.

"Give me your till," Luke growled.

The boy turned to the cash register, slammed a key, and the drawer slid out with a ring. He grabbed the inside of the drawer with both hands, yanked it out and pushed it over the counter to Luke. Luke picked up the gun and slipped it into his pocket. Then he looked at the drawer on the counter and pulled out the blue bag.

The Porky Pig mask had small eyeholes, and Luke had to tilt his head down to see the cash drawer. As he did he heard scrambling. He jerked his head up to see the attendant grabbing at a back door. Luke yanked the gun out of his pocket and pointed it at the boy as he got the door open. The scene seemed frozen and quiet, almost like a bull ride. Luke's finger tightened on the trigger.

Then the boy was through the door, sprinting into the night.

"Damn," Luke snarled, lowering the gun. He stuffed it back in his jacket. Then he quickly dumped the contents of the drawer into the bag, noticing that quarters and nickels were bouncing on the floor. He tossed the drawer back over the counter and lunged out the door. As he leapt over the step onto the wet asphalt, he heard a siren nearby. He ripped off the mask and dashed around the corner of the station. He made it to the alley and ran away from the sound of the closing siren. He jumped over a fence into a back-yard and ran to the side of the house and kicked open the gate. He sprinted across the road and disappeared into a tangle of dark streets.

"Man, you rode like a madman out there today." Harvey and Luke were standing near the wall of the Williams Lake Hall. "Second place!" Harvey went on. "That Angus bull you drew really went to work for you."

Luke pulled on his beer and looked at the crowd. It was Saturday night. The rodeo was over, but not the party. Hundreds of cowboys and cowboy wannabes jammed the place. A twangy country and western band was playing on a raised stage at the front of the hall. Actually, it was the outdoor ice rink with 10-foot walls around it. Luke could see the stars in the clear night sky overhead.

"Yeah, I like those short, solid bulls."

"You must. Eighty-eight points is good, damned good."

"I wanted to win, though. That's what I wanted," Luke muttered, tilting his beer back.

"Hey, you made 500 bucks. What do you want?" Harvey pounded the front of his shirt. "Look at me. I'm out my entry fee for the fourth straight week. How am I going to get to Kamloops? And I've gotta be there. That's the Provincials."

Suddenly there was a scream on the dance floor. Luke's head whipped around, and he saw a woman stagger toward an exit with blood streaming down her face from a gash in her forehead. Another scream rose over the music. Then two more.

"What the hell's going on, Harvey?"

"Look." Harvey pointed up into the sky. When Luke looked up he saw a beer bottle fly over the walls. It smashed on the cement floor six feet away. Glass sprayed across the floor. Suddenly four or five more bottles came hurtling over the walls. One glanced off the back of a guy just a few feet away from Harvey and Luke.

"Jesus," Luke said. "This is nuts."

Now the dance floor was filled with yelling and screaming. People inside started throwing bottles back over the walls. In front, the band played on, indifferent to the wounded on the dance floor.

Luke drained the last of his beer and grabbed it by the neck. "I don't know about you, Harvey," he said, heading for the exit. "But I'm gonna kick some butt."

Harvey grinned and leaned against the wall. "I've been beaten up enough today. You go ahead."

Luke joined a surge of angry cowboys heading out the doors. "Chicken!" he yelled back.

"Maybe," Harvey said quietly to himself. "But I'm not crazy like you, you tough little son of a bitch."

4

"If you can get me a 27-inch Sony stereo, I've got a buyer." Buddy Marshall leaned closer to Luke over the table. "I'll give you $200 for it."

"Come on, Buddy," Luke snorted. "That's an 800, 900 dollar set. Don't jerk me around. Three-fifty or forget it."

Buddy was the best fence in town. He had connections with the gangs in Vancouver and could get rid of anything of value. And at top dollar too. But Luke wasn't going to take the risk of getting busted for nothing.

Buddy hesitated. "Three hundred. That's my final offer. Take it or leave it."

Now it was Luke's turn to hesitate. He thought he could pull this off easily, and he needed the money. "OK, $300. When do you need it by?"

"Tomorrow. And remember, its got to be stereo or the whole deal is off."

"OK, OK, stereo it is. I'll have it at your house tomorrow night."

They both sat back in their red vinyl chairs and watched the pool players at the table next to them. Agnes was lining up on the eight ball.

Freddy's was a bit of a dive. The beer parlour had clearly seen better days. The red terry cloth covers on the round tables were stained and torn. The ceiling was dark with cigarette smoke. But Luke knew every one in the place. It was home and family to him. And work too. He could buy guns, dope. Fence stolen goods.

Luke drained the last of the beer in his glass. "If I'm going to have that for you tomorrow, I better get to work." He pushed his chair back and stood up.

"Remember, it's gotta be a Sony." Buddy shook his head. "Everyone's so fussy these days. What's wrong with an RCA?"

Luke opened the door of the pub and blinked in the bright sunlight. He walked to his pickup and climbed in. He noticed the rust around the wheel wells. Hell, there was more rust than paint, he thought. Hardly can tell it's supposed to be white. Maybe after the Provincials I can get this thing painted. If I can score big there, I could make $5,000.

He climbed into the cab and drove downtown. He parked in the Eaton's parking lot. Then he walked up toward the main street. The big department stores all had alarm systems. So did most of the electronics stores. He kept walking until he got to Dabble's Photo store. He walked in. They specialized in cameras, but in one corner they had a few Sony TV's. Luke hoped they had a 27-inch stereo.

"Can I help you?" A middle-aged woman with curly brown hair was smiling at him.

"Oh, no. Thanks. I was just looking. Thinking about getting a new VCR."

"Well, you just let me know if I can be of assistance."

"You bet. I'll do that. Thanks."

Luke browsed through the VCR's and then quickly surveyed the TV's. Yep, there it was. Twenty-seven inches. He squinted at the control panel. Stereo. Bingo.

As he walked along the far wall, he noticed the back door. No alarm wires that he could see. An inside door of metal bars was opened against the wall. A padlock hung from a ring in the door frame. He made his way through the store toward the front entrance. He was careful not to draw attention to himself. He didn't want anyone to remember him.

"Perfect," Buddy said as they unloaded the TV out of the back of Luke's truck into Buddy's garage. "How'd it go?"

"It was cool," Luke replied. "The door wasn't wired. I jimmied the lock. They had a barred inside door that was padlocked. Bolt cutters took care of that."

They eased the set onto boards on the cement floor. Buddy covered it with an old blanket. Other blanket-covered shapes filled the back of the garage.

Luke reached into the cab of his truck. "I grabbed a couple of portable CD players." He held up two black CD and cassette decks. "They're Sonys too."

"That wasn't part of the bargain." Buddy's tone was sharp, cold.

Luke's temper flared. "Listen, you creep. If you don't want them, fine. I'll find somebody who does."

"All right, all right. Calm down. I'll give you a hundred for the pair."

Luke glowered at Buddy and put the CD players on top of the TV. Buddy pulled out his wallet and leafed through the bills. He pulled out four 100's and handed them to Luke.

"Square?"

Luke nodded curtly. He took the money and examined it carefully.

Buddy laughed. "Do you really think I'd try to pass counterfeits to a business associate, Luke? How stupid do you think I am?"

Luke slipped the money into his pocket and climbed into his truck. Buddy pushed a button on a console he held in one hand. The door slid open, and Luke drove out.

Luke was watching wrestling and eating macaroni and cheese from the pot he'd fixed it in. He had an open beer on the small folding table next to the recliner. There was a knock at his apartment door. Luke glanced at his watch—9:30 p.m. Who the hell could that be?

He put the pot on the table and stood up slowly. He looked around the apartment. No guns, no dope in sight. The knock came at the door again, this time louder.

"Yeah, yeah, I'm coming," Luke called.

He walked to the door and looked through the peephole. Two

uniformed RCMP officers stood in the hall. One had his hand on the butt of his holstered pistol.

Shit, thought Luke. What do I do now? He thought about the window, but he was on the second floor. One of the cops hammered on the door. "Open up or we're coming in. We have a warrant and a pass key."

Luke reluctantly twisted the bolt on the door. He opened it up about 12 inches.

"Yeah. What do you guys want?"

"Luke Tronson?"

"Maybe. Why?"

"Because you are under arrest for breaking and entering and theft over $500."

Luke started to shut the door. "You must have the wrong guy."

One of the cops stuck his foot in the doorway. "I don't think so. We staked out Buddy Marshall's place and got your plate number. Besides, Buddy squealed. Back away from the door."

That slimy son of a bitch, Luke thought angrily. You can't trust anyone anymore.

"Come on," said a Mountie, taking him by the arm. "You're doing time for this one."

Luke tore free from his grip. "I can't!" he yelled. "This weekend is the Provincials!"

"You should have thought of that before you broke into Dabble's," the cop said. "The only provincial you're going to be in this weekend is a provincial jail."

5

"No, man. You never wear one of those plastic masks when you're pulling a robbery. You can't see out of them."

Luke was sitting with Pappy White in the recreation room of the Kamloops jail. They were playing cribbage.

"Ski masks are the best," Pappy went on. "You know those knitted masks with holes for your eyes and mouth. You pull them over your head. They don't obstruct your vision."

Luke put his cards down and stared out the window.

"You gonna play?" Luke gave no response. "Hey, forget about the damned rodeo, will you? You only got six months. You'll be out before next season. You can go next year."

Luke looked at Pappy. He was a chunky man with a thin moustache and scraggly beard.

"Why don't you shave, Pappy?"

"It would ruin my disguise."

"Who are you pretending to be?"

"A tough B and E artist with a funny name."

Luke gave a short laugh. "That's no disguise. That's who you are."

"Nah. Actually I'm a marshmallow underneath. The kind of guy that helps little old ladies across the street."

"Yeah," Luke agreed. "And steals their purses in the process."

Pappy wrinkled his forehead and looked sad. "Luke, I am hurt. Deeply wounded. I've never stolen a little old lady's purse in my life."

"Only because you haven't had the chance. Where did you get the name Pappy?"

Pappy shrugged. "Real name's Pepe. My mom heard it somewhere and thought it was exotic. Nobody could pronounce it. Started calling me Pappy. Anybody calls me Pepe now gets a fat lip."

Luke looked up at the clock. "Man, I'm tired. I worked all day in that damned kitchen."

"Could be worse. Could be out slashing in the bush like me. At least you're learning a trade."

"Yeah, I'm learning to be a prison cook. That way they won't have to retrain me every time I come back."

"Listen, this place is easy. Take it from me. This is a summer camp compared to Okalla." Pappy's face clouded. "Stay clear of that place."

"I'll keep that advice in mind. What's going on tonight? I heard Sammy talking about some new guy in our dorm." Pappy and Luke were in "D" dorm set aside for prisoners doing between six and nine months.

Pappy put his cards on the table and took the markers out of the crib board. He picked up the heavy wooden piece and held it in his large right hand. It looked like a hammer. Pappy lowered his voice.

"Word is they've put a wife beater in here. Beat her up bad. Put her in the hospital. Broken jaw, concussion. May have lost the sight of one eye."

"Son of a bitch," Luke hissed. "Who the hell would hit a woman? What kind of lousy excuse for a man would put a woman in the hospital?"

"Guess we'll find out tonight. We're going to give him a little greeting from the boys of D dorm after lights are out."

"Count me in."

The lights were turned out at 10:00 p.m. An hour later, Luke felt someone tap his foot. He rolled silently out of bed and grabbed a running shoe. He could see five or six figures in the darkness. Sammy carried a blanket. Pappy had the cribbage board.

At this time of night only two guards were on duty. Both were outside the dorm in the lit duty room. One was working on a file on the desk. Luke couldn't see the other one.

Sammy took them down the row of 40 bunk beds until they got to the far end of the dorm. Bunk 20A. This was the guy. He tossed uneasily in his lower bed.

Suddenly Sammy sprang forward and covered the man's head with the blanket. He jammed the palm of his hand over the man's mouth. Luke could hear muffled yells. The other men moved in.

They began punching the man writhing in bed. Luke heard Pappy bring the cribbage board down on the man's head. It hit with a dull thud. The yells turned to screams.

The beating went on for five or six minutes. No one in the rest of the bunks stirred during the entire time. Finally the man underneath the blanket stopped squirming. Only a few low sobs indicated that the man was still alive. Sammy motioned the men back. They moved to their bunks as silently as they had come.

Some time later Luke heard the beaten man lurch to the washroom. He heard him vomit and wash the blood away. He knew one of the guards would find the blood the next morning. He would see the cuts and bruises on the man they had beaten. But he had seen no one, even if he was stupid enough to talk. The guards would ask a few questions. The warden might reprimand the dorm. That would be it. He fell asleep, his face set in grim satisfaction.

6

It was the Sunday of the Vernon rodeo. Luke had been out of jail for five months. He was determined to stay out. He couldn't win the Provincials from jail. Social Services had helped him find a job at a restaurant. It wasn't much—just a small fish and chips place. But the owner let him off on weekends so he could ride.

And ride he did. He had done better than ever. He had piled up points that again put him in the top 10 bull riders in the province. He was glad he hadn't had to travel this weekend. The eight dollars an hour he was getting at the restaurant wasn't going very far. He was struggling each week for the entry fees. Not to mention the travel expenses.

But at least he was winning some purses. In the bull riding finals earlier, he had gone in fourth. He needed to make a good ride to get into the money. He had drawn Topper. Topper was a short Black Angus cross with a nasty disposition. Luke had never ridden him. Before the ride he asked around. Paul Bannon had drawn him the week before in Cranbrook.

"He's so short he's dangerous," Paul had told him. "He can turn on a dime. Likes to go into spins. And watch out for him coming out of the chute. He likes to rear up when the gates open."

Topper had been restless in the chutes. He banged Luke's legs against the boards until he could get set. Luke was hurting before he even got out of the gate. Luke wrapped his gloved right hand into the rigging and pulled it deep into the black back of the bull. "Chute!"

As soon as the gate opened the Angus reared upwards. At the same time he twisted sharply to the right, slamming Luke's right shoulder against the edge of the chute. The pain shot down his arm. But Luke was ready. He sat tight against his hand lashed to the bull's back. His left hand was tugging hair. Then they were clear of the chute. The Angus spun to the left with surprising agility. He raked the bull across the right shoulder with his spurs. He put all of the strength in his right arm, yanking right.

The bull straightened, snorting and bucking. Then it pulled to the right. Luke straightened him out before he could get into a full spin. Topper twisted across the arena. His rear end went one way and his front the other. But Luke held on until the horn cut through the silence of the ride.

Luke released the rigging and leapt clear of the bull. Just as his boots touched the dirt he felt the kicking feet of the bull whistle by his temple. Then the clown distracted it. Topper went kicking and bucking harmlessly across the arena.

Luke picked up his hat and knocked the dust off on his chaps. He put it on his head and walked to the boards and climbed over.

He heard the crowd cheer as he jumped onto the ground. His score flashed on the board—92! One of his best rides ever.

And it had been enough to move him into second place.

So now he and Harvey were heading for the Jade Palace for dinner. Luke was buying.

"Did you see that newspaper guy?" Harvey asked. "He got some great shots of you taking Topper to the cleaners."

"Yeah. He came up later and had me sign some releases."

"You're a star!"

"I'm a second place star." Suddenly Luke looked up the street and stopped. "Aw, shit."

Harvey stopped too. "What's wrong?"

Luke nodded up the street. "It's that jerk Bobby and his stooge Willy. They're standing right in front of the Jade Palace." Harvey noticed a big guy in a black leather coat leaning up against the plate glass window with "Jade Palace" painted on it. He was smoking a cigarette.

"So what? It's a free country."

"Freer for some than others. Bobby has wanted me dead ever since we pulled a B and E four years ago. I got nabbed and then they picked him up. He thinks I snitched. I didn't. Harvey, I'm not interested in a fight tonight."

"Come on." Harvey started up the street again. "He's probably forgotten all about it."

Luke followed reluctantly. As they neared the restaurant the man in the black leather coat looked up. His small eyes were set too close together. They flickered from Luke to Harvey. Then they settled on Luke.

"Well, look who's here. My little buddy Luke. And I do mean little." Bobby dropped his cigarette on the sidewalk. He ground it out with the heel of his cowboy boot. His face was illuminated by the light coming from the window. He smiled cruelly. He looked at Willy, who was standing in the doorway. "Actually, Willy, he's a little faggot. Aren't you, Luke?"

Luke ignored Bobby and began to walk around him. Bobby shot out a hand and grabbed the front of Luke's shirt. Luke tensed.

"I'm not interested in a fight, Bobby," Luke said quietly.

"Did you hear that, Willy? The little faggot doesn't want to fight. Too bad he doesn't take after his father. He was a drunk, but at least he was man enough to fight. And at least he didn't rat."

Luke felt the rage rise in him like fire.

" 'Course, the only people his mother fought with were welfare workers and—"

Luke uncoiled like a tight spring. He pivoted to the right. His arm came up and knocked Bobby's grip from his shirt. At the same time his left hand hooked into the bigger man's nose. Blood gushed across his face. Luke brought his left knee sharply into the man's crotch. As he doubled over in pain, Luke brought his other knee up to Bobby's chin.

Bobby's head snapped back and he fell heavily against the window. The glass exploded inward. The shards glittered like crystals. Bobby lay on the floor inside on a bed of broken glass. His legs hanging over the sharp edges of the window. Blood was dripping down onto the floor. Luke looked up from the man on the floor. A small blonde woman in a waitress uniform was standing with her fists on her hips looking at him angrily.

"Who's going to clean this up?" she demanded.

Harvey brushed Willy aside and grabbed the door handle. "Excuse us. We were about to have dinner. You and Bobby care to join us?"

Luke realized that customers inside were standing around the figure on the floor. Bobby was groaning. Blood was flowing from several cuts on his face and head. He heard a siren whine in the distance. He got set to run. Then he looked up at the woman in the window. She was still staring at him. But this time there was something else there. Something besides anger. Something softer.

She seemed to sense that he was ready to run. "Don't." She said. "I saw it all. I'll tell the cops how he grabbed you. It was self defense."

Luke relaxed and waited for the police. And for the woman in the window.

"I want to thank you. I never did get your name." Luke was walking the Jade Palace waitress across the road to her car. He had his arm around her shoulders.

"Well, we didn't get a lot of opportunity to chat."

First the ambulance had come and pulled Bobby out of the glass. Blood had been everywhere. Then the police had come. Luke looked up as they came in the door with a start. It was the same two that had arrested him 11 months before.

They looked around at the mess on the floor and then at Luke. "Looks like you just couldn't get enough of jail, eh Luke?" one said. "Can't wait to get back, eh?"

Luke's eyes narrowed. He started to reply.

"You got this wrong, officer," the waitress had cut in. "The bigger guy started it."

The police looked around doubtfully. "Anybody else see it?"

Harvey stood up from a booth nearby. "I saw the whole thing. It's just like she said."

The police looked at each other and shrugged. They wrote up the details and interviewed some of the customers. All the stories cleared Luke. After half an hour they left.

"It's Belinda," the woman said finally. "Belinda Walker. Call me Bel for short."

"You're not that short," Luke said.

They were nearing her car parked behind the restaurant. Luke let his hand drop down her back and rest on the round rise of her buttocks. Bel whirled around and drove her right fist into Luke's mouth. He sat down hard on the asphalt. Blood was spilling from a split lip.

"You don't want to piss around with me, Luke Tronson," she said. She continued across the lot and got into her car. Luke was slowly getting to his feet as she drove out of the lot.

"But if you're going to behave yourself, give me a call." She leaned out of the window and handed him a scrap of paper. Then she drove away.

7

"Why do you hang around in a crummy place like this, Luke?" Bel looked up at the stained ceiling of Freddy's. A guy with a three-day beard and a sweat-stained Caterpillar hat on his head sat hunched over a beer at the bar. "You're better than this. You deserve better than this."

Luke looked darkly into his glass. "What do you know about me?" he said. "You don't know anything. Besides, what's wrong with this place?"

"Well, the ceiling tiles are falling down. The floor looks like it hasn't been cleaned in months. The chairs are all ripped. It stinks of cigarette smoke. And the place is full of losers."

"Lay off the people in here," Luke muttered. "They're my friends."

"Luke, wake up for Christ's sake!" Bel hissed. "They're dope pushers. They're crooks. They're people who have given up!"

Luke looked glumly at the few people clustered around the small round tables in the gloomy interior. "They're family."

"But they're *not* your family. You never talk about your family.

How the hell am I going to get to know you if you never talk to me?"

Luke had been taking Bel out almost every night for the last three weeks since the fight. She had to work on weekends, so she didn't go to the rodeos. But every other night they went somewhere and talked.

Talk didn't come easy to Luke. "What do you want, Bel?" he said, peering back into his glass. "What do you want from me?"

"Just tell me one thing about your past. One story about your family. Something, Luke. I like you. I like you a lot. But we're going nowhere if you can't learn to open up with me."

Luke picked up his glass and looked at it. There was about an inch of beer in the bottom. He quickly drank it.

"You want a story about my family? OK, I'll tell you one." He put the glass back on the table. He held it loosely in his right hand. "I was about 11 or 12, I guess. My dad had started raising rabbits. He'd been into everything—logging, bartending, farming. He'd been a bouncer in a pub. Big guy. Couldn't keep anything together. He started the day with a 26-er of rye. Then he'd suck on another bottle all day. He always had one in his back pocket. He finished off the day with eight or 10 beers. But somehow he'd gotten enough money together to fix up the old barn and buy these rabbits. We had about 5,000 of them, I guess. All in cages."

Luke rolled the empty glass slowly in his hand. "So this one day my brother goes into the rabbit barn. He must have been seven or eight, I guess. I'm busy cleaning, doing my chores at the other end. Don't really pay any attention to him. Suddenly I hear him yell. I turn and look and smoke is filling up the whole far end of the barn. He's been playing with matches and managed to start the hay on fire."

Luke stopped, studied the glass in his hand.

"So what did you do?" asked Bel.

"I ran down and tried to put the fire out. First I tried to use old burlap feed sacks to smother it. I burned my hands. Singed off my eyebrows. But that was useless. The flames raced up the old wood and into the roof. The whole place went up in minutes."

"Did you lose everything?"

Luke nodded. "Every single rabbit. My dad came running up while Louie, my brother, and I were standing watching the fire. Dad had a garden hose in his hand. But the fire was way too far gone for that. He started squirting the fire. But even he saw nothing could be done. Then he turned to me.

"He slashed the brass nozzle across my face. Then he grabbed me by the hair and yanked my head back until I thought my neck was going to break. He stuck the hose into my mouth, the water still running, until I choked. I felt like I was drowning. I was gagging, but he kept pouring the water in. I tried to scream. Finally he stopped. I fell to the ground. I was retching, throwing up. Sobbing."

There were tears in Bel's eyes. "But you didn't do anything! It wasn't your fault! Why didn't you tell him the truth?"

"I never rat. Not ever. And it didn't matter anyway. I was the oldest. He hated me. I never really knew why. So he threw me in a shack out back of the house where we kept the old tractor and locked the door. I stayed there for a week and a half. He brought in an old mattress and I got one meal a day. And when he brought it in he beat me with his razor strap. On the face, the arms, my back. He just lashed out in fury for what seemed like forever. He screamed at me. Called me everything you can think of. Blamed me for ruining him. That went on for a week and a half."

Tears were rolling down Bel's cheeks. Luke's left hand was clenched in a fist on the red cloth table top. She put her hand over it gently.

He jerked his hand back savagely and flung the glass he had in his other hand on the floor. It smashed on the dirty linoleum.

"So there's a story from my past, lady," he said fiercely. His eyes were blazing as he glared at her over the table. "Don't tell me who I am and what I am." He spit out the words. "You don't know me. You don't know me at all."

Bel pulled her empty hand back and sat staring at him.

"I'm sorry, Luke. I really am."

Luke took a deep, shuddering breath. "Come on," he said in a softer voice. "Let me take you home."

"OK, but Luke?"

"Yeah?"

"I'm not giving up."

Working at Whaler's Fish and Chips was a drag for Luke any day. But this one started out worse than most. Luke had gone in late and sullen. When Larry, the owner, saw him walk into the kitchen, he looked at the clock over the door. Half an hour late. He started to say something. Then he noticed the tension in Luke's jaw, the tight lips. And there was something hard around the eyes. He thought better of it.

"I need these potatoes peeled and sliced right away," Larry said.

Luke said nothing. He put on an apron and moved to the sack of potatoes.

Larry went back to mixing batter. Several minutes later he looked up. Luke was sitting with his empty hands on the counter. He was staring off into space.

Now Larry was irritated. "Luke," he called sharply. "I said I needed those potatoes right away."

Suddenly Luke stood up and yanked off his apron. He turned to Larry. Luke's face was twisted with rage. He hurled the apron onto the kitchen floor.

"Screw you, Larry!" Luke screamed. "And all your goddamned potatoes!" He grabbed one from the sack with his right hand. He lunged forward and threw the potato at Larry's head. The potato missed and smashed into a stack of white plates on the dishwasher. Then Luke spun and headed for the door.

"Luke," Larry called after him. "I don't know what's wrong, but this is no answer. You walk out of here and you're losing a chance to go straight." Luke hesitated in the doorway. "Don't do it."

Luke gave Larry one look over his shoulder. Larry caught only a quick glimpse of Luke's dark eyes. But in that instant he saw rage, sorrow and hopelessness.

Then Luke stormed out of the kitchen. He slammed the front door on the way out.

8

"Pappy, it's me, Luke." Luke stood in the downtown phone booth looking out on the traffic in front of him. "Yeah, it's good to talk to you, too. But, listen, I gotta talk to you in person. In private."

He was quiet while Pappy spoke on the other end.

"OK. How about I meet you halfway. We'll meet in the Patricia Arms pub in Salmon Arm. Yeah, two o'clock is fine. See you then."

Luke hung up the phone and stared blankly out the glass. Finally an old woman with grey hair tapped on the phone booth door. "Young man, are you all right?"

"Huh?" Luke turned toward the door. "Yeah, yeah. I'm fine."

"Well then do you mind getting the hell out of there so I can call my grandson for a ride?"

Luke grinned and pushed the door open. He held it open for her and bowed. "It's all yours, lady."

The drive to Salmon Arm took Luke about 45 minutes. He pulled into the parking lot at 1:30. That was OK. He wanted to collect his thoughts before Pappy got there anyway. He opened the heavy wood door and walked into the dim interior.

At this time of day the place was pretty empty. One guy with a cigarette pack rolled into his shirt sleeve shot alone on the pool table. A couple of older guys sat watching a baseball game near the front. Luke headed for a table in the far corner near the dance floor. There was no one to overhear.

As he sat down a barmaid walked up to the table. She wore a blue shirt with "Pat Pub" embroidered on the pocket.

"What can I get for you, cowboy."

Luke realized he still had his hat on. He quickly took it off and tossed it onto an empty chair next to him. "Uh, a Blue will be fine."

After the woman left, Luke took out a small spiral bound notebook and pencil. He began to write the names of businesses in Vernon. He crossed some off. He circled others.

He was still studying his notebook when Pappy walked up to the table.

"Luke, good to see you."

Luke looked up and shook Pappy's hand. "Sit down. Can I buy you a beer?"

Pappy sat in the chair next to Luke. "What's up, Luke? You didn't call me over here for a beer."

Luke lowered his voice. "I need money. Not just enough to get by. Some real money. I'm talking $100,000. I want to clean out Vernon."

Pappy nodded towards Luke's notebook. "You got a plan?"

Luke opened the book up and pushed it towards Pappy. "I

know that city. I've been through every business in the place. Here are 11 we can knock over easily. I put question marks by the ones with a security system."

"No problem. I can bring in Toots." Toots was Pappy's sometime partner. Luke had met him in the Kamloops jail. "There isn't a system made Toots can't get around."

Luke nodded. "OK. Then there will be the three of us. I've listed the places from south to north." He flipped a page. "And here's a rough map. I figure we can start here," Luke pointed to a circle with a number one in it. "It's a lawyer's office. They just got in a brand new batch of computers. Eight, maybe 10 of them."

Luke's finger traced a zigzag path through the town. "And by four in the morning we'll be here." He pointed to another circle on the north edge of town, marked 11.

Pappy looked puzzled. "That's a cement plant. What do they have?"

"Money for one thing. I was in there. They've got wads of money on Friday in a little cash box. They lock it in a file cabinet. They've also got cutting torches. Welders. All kinds of tools."

Pappy was nodding again. "OK. So we'll need a truck. And moving dollies. I'll rent them from Kamloops. It'll be harder to trace. I'll drive over Friday during the day with Toots."

"So you're in?"

Pappy pulled the thin goatee on his chin. "Yeah. I'm in."

"Good. But Pappy," Luke said.

"Yeah?"

"This is it for me. I've met a woman. I want to get this money and set us up. Maybe a business. Maybe go back to school. I don't know. But I know her. She's not going to put up with me going in and out of jail."

Pappy grinned. "So a woman has shown you the error of your ways. Something the jails couldn't do, eh?"

"The only thing the jails did was introduce me to crooks like you," Luke said, smiling. "You taught me everything I know."

Pappy tipped a pretend hat. "You flatter me. I'm just glad I could help out."

Luke poured the last of the Blue into his glass and drank it. "So I'll see you and Toots at my apartment on Friday. Around five?"

Pappy nodded. "Friday at five."

They pulled into Johnson Brothers Concrete at about 4:45 a.m. The van was almost full. Computers, TV's, small safes, furniture, VCR's, answering machines, and calculators were jammed to the top. The van lights were out and the parking lot seemed eerie. Huge cement trucks hulked in the darkness. Only a single light shone in front of the small office at the far end of the lot.

Luke was sitting by the van window. Toots was next to him and Pappy was driving. So far things had gone smoothly. Only the Greyhound station had been a problem. When they broke through the back door the alarm had sounded for a few seconds before Toots could knock it out. They had just had time to grab a small floor safe after jimmying the door to the office. Then they fled. Toots wasn't sure if a signal had gone into the security company or not.

Now Luke was getting nervous. He'd never been nervous before. Not even during his first job. But something didn't feel right. Pappy had pulled up to the main office and was backing the van up to the front door.

"Pappy," Luke said quietly. "We've got more stuff than we know what to do with. Let's skip this place and get the hell out of here."

Pappy was looking behind them through the side view mirror.

"No way, Luke my boy," he said, still looking out his window. "This is the reason we're doing this on Friday, remember? The cash box in the file cabinet?"

Pappy had stopped the van.

"Yeah," Luke went on. "But we're nearly an hour behind schedule. It'll be light in another hour."

Pappy put the transmission in park. He set the brake and left the motor running. "This won't take long. Come on."

He opened the driver side door and got out. Luke hesitated.

"Come on, Luke. Move it," Pappy hissed from outside. "I need Toots."

Reluctantly Luke pulled the door handle and opened the door. He stepped out onto the asphalt. It was wet and slick with early morning dew.

Toots pushed by him and walked quickly over to the door. He carried a small tool kit. Pappy was already studying the door closely.

"Looks like a simple external alarm," Toots muttered, tracing wires to a red bell under the eaves of the roof. He took out a pair of wire cutters and began snipping. In the quiet Luke could hear the low snap as the wires were cut.

"OK," Toots whispered. "That should do it. Come on Luke!"

Luke shook his head and frowned. He grabbed the crowbar from the floor of the van and moved to the door. Pappy and Toots were waiting for him impatiently. He expertly inserted the crow bar between the door and jam. He moved it down the door until it was by the handle. Then he pried. There was a sharp snap. Toots kicked the bottom of the door. It swung inward. Toots and Pappy rushed in.

Pappy pulled a flashlight out of his coat and began to shine it around the office.

"Luke! Get in here! Where the hell is that box?"

Luke walked into the office and brought out his own flashlight. He shone the light on a bank of three grey file cabinets behind a large wood desk. He moved the light to the top drawer of the far cabinet.

"It's this one."

Luke followed his flashlight beam to the cabinet. He inserted the tip of his crowbar into the top of the drawer and pulled. The drawer rolled out toward them.

Pappy rushed up and yanked the drawer out all the way. He reached into the back and pulled out a tan cash box.

Suddenly there was a squeal of tires and a shrieking of sirens. Flashing red lights cut through the darkness. "Damn it!" Toots cursed. "There must have been another alarm."

Pappy dashed for the open door. Luke dropped his crowbar

and ran after Pappy. As soon as he got outside he saw police cars pouring into the parking lot.

"There's no other way out," Pappy yelled. "Split up and run!"

Pappy headed for the line of cement trucks on the other side of the lot. Luke felt Toots shove by him and follow Pappy. The police cars were only 30 metres away now. The sirens were deafening. Luke saw the only way out was to run behind the building into the brush. He clicked off his flashlight and sprinted around the corner of the office.

Headlights and spotlights were sweeping the parking lot. Luke made it to the high grass. He ran a few more feet and fell into a deep ditch. The highway was above him on the other side of the ditch. If he could hide here until the cops left he might make it. He lay flat in the dry grass at the bottom of the ditch. He tried to quiet his ragged breathing.

Luke lay in the ditch for what seemed like hours. Actually, it was probably more like 15 or 20 minutes. The sky began to lighten. He heard yells from the police. Orders being given. The crackling of radios. Doors slamming. Cars driving away. Luke looked up at the edge of the ditch. It seemed clear. He needed to know what was going on. He crawled up the bank. He slowly stuck his head up.

Two cops stood six feet away, guns drawn. They looked right at him. One shined a powerful flashlight beam in his eyes. Luke was blinded.

"Halt!" one of the cops yelled. "You're under arrest! Put your hands over your head and stand up slowly!'

Still blinking from the flashlight, Luke did as he was told. The cop holding the flashlight also had a gun on him. The other grabbed Luke's right arm and roughly yanked it behind his back. He snapped a handcuff on Luke's wrist. Then he yanked the other arm down and clicked the other cuff around his left wrist.

The man with the flashlight walked up and pointed the beam into Luke's face. "Well, let's see who we've got here."

Luke groaned. It was the same cop that had arrested him for the TV. The same one that had investigated the fight.

The cop stared into Luke's face as he tried to turn away from the blinding light.

"We got you this time, eh Tronson?" Luke said nothing. "But there's a difference this time," the cop continued. Luke could see him sneering.

Luke twisted the other way. He was trying to get away from the sharp beam of the flashlight. It was jabbing into his eyes like daggers. Luke tried to spit at the cop in front of him. The other man yanked the handcuffs upward. Luke screamed in pain.

The cop with the flashlight stuck his face close to Luke's. "Here's the difference, you little creep. No more Camp Kamloops. This round you're doing hard time."

He lowered the flashlight. The other RCMP officer shoved him toward the waiting car.

9

Bel sat on one side of the table in the Vernon jail. She was crying and twisting a tissue in her hand. Luke leaned over the table toward Bel. A police officer stood a few feet away.

"So they're sending you to Okalla tomorrow," Bel said softly.

"Yeah, I guess so."

Bel broke into tears. "Oh, Luke, you're so stupid! Why did you have to talk back to the judge?"

Luke sat back in his chair remembering the day before, at the trial. His legal aid lawyer hadn't held out much hope: "With your record…" He shrugged. "Maybe I can make a deal with the prosecutor. Get you off with 12 months. That'll keep you in Kamloops."

And then the judge had pronounced the sentence: two years in Okalla.

Luke had felt fury, betrayal. He felt fear. He had lunged up from his chair in the courtroom. "Two years," he had sneered. "I can do that standing on my head!"

The judge looked up, startled. Then his face clouded. He leaned forward over his bench. "Well, then, Mr. Tronson, I'd better give you another six months to get back on your feet." He looked at the court reporter. "Make that 30 months in Okalla."

Luke shook his head at the memory. Bel was right. Stupid. Really stupid.

"Bel," he started hesitantly. "I know this doesn't make sense." Bel kept looking down at the table, twisting her tissue. "But, well, I like you. I, I wanted to try to make a life with you. I didn't know how else to do it."

Now Bel glared at Luke. Her red eyes were hard. "Luke Tronson, don't give me that crap. Don't tell me you did this for *us*," she hissed. "What I wanted for us was a relationship. Love. Caring. You're so caught up in your own pain you can't see anything!" Bel blew her nose.

"Don't you see?" she went on. "I don't like you because of how much money you have. Or how many belt buckles you win. And I sure don't care about you because you're a big macho crook." She paused until Luke looked at her. "I love you because of who you are. Don't you get it? Who you are inside. And that's a caring and decent guy."

Luke looked away. The silence dragged on for several seconds.

"Will you wait for me?" Luke asked, still not looking at her.

"No, Luke, I won't wait for you," Bel said evenly. "I'm not going to put my whole life on hold for two and a half years."

Luke nodded. "I understand."

"No you don't, Luke. I'm not saying I won't still be here. I'm not saying that I don't love you. Or that I'm not willing to give you another chance. I'm saying that I won't wait for the person who breaks into buildings. Who holds up gas stations. Who thinks he has to get respect by riding bulls. I'm not interested in that person."

Luke looked back at Bel. She was speaking softly, even kindly.

"Well what then?"

"I'm not going to wait for the person going in. You don't deserve it." Luke hung his head. "But I may wait and see who comes out."

Luke sat staring at the grey top of the desk. "Will you come visit me?"

Bel hesitated. "I don't know," she said. "I'm not promising anything. I'll see."

The police officer looked at the clock on the wall.

"OK, Miss. Time's up. You'll have to leave now."

Luke reached across the table and took her hand. "You mean more to me than anyone I've ever known." He said it simply, truthfully. He squeezed her hand and stood up. He turned around and walked through the door to the cells. He didn't look back.

Luke couldn't actually see the prison from the back of the sheriff's car. Instead he saw the massive grey stone walls that surrounded Okalla. They were at least 15 feet high. The car pulled up to huge wooden gates set into the wall. A guard came out from a small building and looked at the sheriff's papers. He asked a few questions and gave the papers back. He stepped back into the guard house and opened the gates. He motioned the car forward.

The wooden gates swung inward. Luke felt like he was being

sucked inside. Like Jonah and the whale. He was being swallowed whole. The car drove in. Luke turned his head and watched the gates swing shut.

When he looked forward he saw another stone wall in front of him. This one was almost as high as the outside wall. Rolls of razor wire stretched across the top. Green guard towers were at each corner. They drove up to another gate. This one was metal. It swung open and they drove on. As they passed through the second gate a cloud darkened the sun. Luke looked up and saw guards walking along the inside of the wall on catwalks. They carried rifles. The gate clanged behind him. He remembered the cop's words: "This round you're doing hard time."

Inside the second set of walls there were several brown buildings. Behind them there was a 12-foot chain-link fence. More razor wire was rolled across the top. Ten feet back was another fence. Luke saw the black shapes of dogs pacing nervously in between the two fences. Inside these he saw the dorms. There were five of them. Each was four tiers high. There were bars on all the windows. Rows and rows of barred windows.

The car stopped at a building outside of the fences. A sign over the door said "Administration." Luke saw several other men being escorted into the building from a police van. They had shackles on their feet and wrists.

The sheriff stopped the car. He got out and opened Luke's door. "OK, partner. This is it."

Luke was handcuffed. He grabbed the door handles with both hands and stepped awkwardly out of the back seat. He looked up at the high wall stretching all around him. The dogs barked and growled behind the fence. Luke knew he was here to stay.

The sheriff opened the door to the office. "Welcome to the Okalla Hilton."

10

Inside the administration building the sheriff unlocked Luke's cuffs. He took his papers to the clerk at the front desk. Luke heard a buzz to his right. A guard came out of a grey steel door. He picked up a clipboard of papers from the clerk. He looked at them briefly and walked up to Luke.

"Through the door," the guard ordered curtly. There was another buzz. The guard pulled the door open. Luke walked into a long dark hallway. Signs with numbers stuck out from the green walls by each door. He could smell disinfectant. Alcohol.

The guard stayed behind him. "Room 4."

Room 4 was halfway down the hall. He stopped by the door. The guard opened it and motioned him forward. Luke walked in.

The room looked like a doctor's office. There were even a few old magazines on a small table. Five or six other men were sitting in chairs. No one even glanced up as he entered. A woman in a white uniform sat writing at a desk. The guard brought the clipboard up to the desk. The woman took it and hung it from a hook on the wall behind her. The guard walked back out into the hallway. Luke heard the door click shut behind him.

Luke sat down and stared at the brown squares of linoleum on the floor. Occasionally a man in an open lab coat would come out and take a clipboard from the wall. Then a buzzer sounded and the woman called a name. The man called walked through a door with frosted glass.

After nearly half an hour, Luke's name was called. He opened the door. There was an examination table against one wall. A single chair sat in a corner. Two doors were in the far wall. One was grey metal. The other had the same frosted glass as the door he had entered. This door opened. The man in the white lab coat walked in. He was writing on one of the clipboards.

"Strip down to your shorts," the man ordered. He didn't even look up.

Luke hesitated. "Are you a doctor?"

The man yanked his eyes up from the papers he was carrying. "What do I look like, a butcher?" he asked. "Get those clothes off. I don't have all day. Then up on the exam table."

Luke didn't much like doctors. He had seen enough of them over the years. There was hardly a bone in his body that he hadn't broken bull riding. But he didn't like the power they had. Their distance. Their coolness.

Luke took off his clothes and sat on the white paper that covered the table. It crinkled underneath him.

The doctor probed and jabbed. He poked at old scars on Luke's shoulders and knees. He looked into Luke's eyes and peered into his ears. Other than to order Luke to cough or say "Ah" with his tongue out, the doctor never said a word. He jotted notes on the clipboard.

Finally the doctor walked back toward the door he'd entered through. He was still writing on the clipboard. He turned.

"OK, Tronson. Through the grey door."

"What about my clothes?"

"Take them with you."

Luke stood up and picked up his pile of clothes. The linoleum was cold on his bare feet. He walked to the metal door and pulled it open.

Inside was another waiting room. Men in their shorts sat along the walls. A long counter stretched across the front. Several guards stood behind the counter. Behind them Luke saw a large shower room.

"Tronson!" one of the guards shouted. "Up front. Now!"

Luke took his clothes up to the counter. The guard took his worn jeans, shirt and cowboy boots and put them into a black plastic bag.

"You won't be needing these for a while, eh cowboy?" The guard gave Luke a big smile. Luke could see his yellow teeth. "Here's soap and a towel."

Luke took them and sat down. A few more men came in.

The other guard looked up. "Prisoners into the shower!" he ordered. "Drop your shorts into the hamper on the way in."

Luke lined up with the other men. They walked around the counter while the guard looked on. Luke pulled his shorts off and dropped them into a cloth hamper outside the entrance to the showers. He walked across the wet tile to the shower in the far corner. As he did, a large man brushed by him. Luke looked up as the other man reached the shower before him. The man had the head of a leopard tattooed on his upper arm. He had long brown hair that fell greasily onto his shoulders. His legs were spindly. Fat settled in a ring around his hips.

As he turned on the water, he looked at Luke. "My shower, chump."

Luke glared at him. The man stared back. Finally Luke walked across the room to an open shower. He faced the tiled wall to turn on the shower. He held the soap in his right hand.

"Hey, Wally. Look at that little turd over there." It was the man with the tattoo behind him.

Luke kept staring at the wall.

"Man, if he was any scrawnier they'd put him in a chicken coop rather than a cell."

Luke said nothing.

"Which might be a good place for him since he's a skinny little chicken shit."

Luke felt his grip tighten around the hard bar of soap.

The man behind him was clearly enjoying himself. "He's so bowlegged I bet he has to press his pants in a circle." Luke heard one of the other men guffaw.

"But you know, Wally. He does have a cute little ass. He looks kind of like a girl from the back, don't you think so, Wally?"

Luke spun and hurled the bar of soap. It caught the man full on his cheek. His head snapped around, his eyes showing surprise and pain. Before he could recover, Luke lunged across the shower room. He brought up a hard left into the man's midsection. He felt his fist bury into the soft, wet flesh. They both crashed against the slippery wall and fell to the floor. The shower head sprayed them as they struggled on the tiled floor.

Other prisoners were yelling encouragement. Luke heard the yells and hooting over the hissing of the water. The tattooed man grabbed Luke by the hair and tried to smash his face against the floor. Luke jerked an elbow hard into his nose. The man yelped and Luke struggled to get to his feet.

Suddenly he felt a hard punch to his temple from above. A strong arm in a blue shirt locked around his neck and yanked upward. One of the guards had him from behind. Luke was choking. A second guard put his boot on the other man's throat. He held a long riot stick in his right hand. It looked like a small baseball bat.

"OK, it's all over!" he yelled. The man on the floor was gasping for air. "Back up against the walls, all of you!" Luke could see the other prisoners in the shower room begin to shuffle back from the fight. "Now!"

The guard yanked the other man up from the floor and pulled his stick roughly against his throat with both hands. Suddenly more guards dashed into the shower room. Luke was almost ready to pass out. Seven, eight guards, maybe more, crowded in. They all had batons in their hands. They forced the other prisoners against the tiled walls. The first two guards then dragged Luke and the other man out of the shower. The guard's arm tightened around Luke's throat. He blacked out.

11

The assistant warden looked over the top of his glasses at Luke.

"So you were here less than an hour and you got into a fight," he said. He looked down through his glasses at the file on his desk. "You are not in Kamloops any more, Mr. Tronson. We won't tolerate that behaviour here. Do you understand?"

Luke sat on a hard wooden chair to the side of the warden's desk. He stared over the warden's right shoulder out the window behind him. The sun shone brightly outside. Two guards stood by the door. Luke said nothing.

"I think we are going to have to drive this point home, Mr. Tronson. You're going to spend the first 10 days of your stay at Okalla in the hole."

Luke kept looking out the window.

The hole—or the digger as they called it in jail—was a block of cells where prisoners were kept in isolation. In Okalla it was located under the cow barns. It was a cement bunker with 10 cells. Each one was five feet wide and eight feet long. There was no window. The only light came through the barred opening in the metal door. The lights outside were on 24 hours a day. The small square let in just a sliver of light. But Luke was grateful for it. It was his sun and his moon. Except when the door was opened twice a day for meals, it was all that saved him from utter darkness.

The only thing to read was the Bible. But since it was almost totally dark, Luke couldn't read even if he wanted to.

Luke wore only his shorts and socks. They had stripped him of his shoes, pants and shirts at the heavy metal door that led to the block of isolation cells. There was a musty feather mattress on the floor. A metal toilet with no seat was bolted to a wall. There was a wash basin next to it.

For 23 of 24 hours Luke stayed in his dark cell. One hour each day a guard let him out. He could walk up and down the narrow walkway that ran the length of the cell block. Maybe 80 feet. A guard with a shotgun stood at the end by the door.

Luke began to panic on the second day. Only his simple breakfast and evening meal told him what time of day it was. The hours stretched on forever. Perhaps they had forgotten him. Surely it was time for dinner. How could he stand the silence, the darkness for 10 days? How could he stand it for 10 minutes?

Luke's heart beat fast. He had trouble breathing. He leapt up from his mattress and shoved his face against the bars of the tiny window in his door. The single bulbs in the ceiling of the walkway gave a dim, harsh light. All he could see was the patch of plain cement in front of him.

Luke felt something break inside. He could hear the shattering.

He was screaming, his face mashed against the six-inch square of light. He could hear his own screams muffled by the low ceiling.

At first there were no words. Just the screams of a trapped, terrified animal. Then words began to form.

"Let me out! I can't take it! Please, someone!"

His cries got weaker. They gave way to sobs. Then he was quiet, his forehead pressed against the bars. His chest was heaving.

Then he thought he heard something. He tried to quiet his breathing. Yes, it was a voice! He turned his left ear to the opening in the door and listened.

"…it easy, partner." The words were weak, muted, but he heard them.

"Is somebody there?" he yelled.

"I'm down here. There's three or four of us. You're not alone." Luke could hardly make out the words. But he could tell the other man was shouting. He must have been several cells away.

Luke shouted back. "What's your name?"

He heard a reply. The cement deadened the sound. It sounded like Mac.

"Mac?" Luke asked.

"Max," the voice corrected him. "Max Cornell. How about you, partner?"

"Luke. Luke Tronson."

"Glad to meet you, Luke. There's Jim a couple of cells down from me. Leo's two cells over from you."

"Yo!" The response came from his right.

Suddenly Luke heard the outside door open. A guard began to walk down the walkway.

"You prisoners shut up!" he yelled "Or else we'll add another 10 days. Got that?"

Luke caught a brief glimpse of the guard through his window. He had a riot club in his hand. His face looked hard, mean. He walked to the end of the walkway and returned. No one said anything. He walked back to the door and left the cell block.

Luke was quiet for several minutes. "Thanks Max," he croaked in a loud whisper. He hoped Max had heard him.

That second day had been the worst. He began to look for other prisoners during their hour exercise break. One gave him a thumbs up sign as he walked by. Luke figured it was Max. He was an older man, maybe 50. He had long grey hair. He smiled as he went by.

The men also managed occasional shouted conversations before the guards shut them up. He got to know Leo. He could barely hear Jim. But he knew he was there. It made the loneliness almost bearable.

Almost. Often Luke found himself crying silently for no reason. Other times he would pound the cement blocks of his cell and scream. Luke had never been so alone. It ate at him. The darkness drained him. But he slept fitfully. Sometimes he would wake up screaming. Other times his eyes would open onto the darkness. He'd panic until he remembered where he was.

One day Max didn't reply to his shouts. Luke figured he had

been taken back to the regular cells. Luke had had seven breakfasts. Three more to go.

"Well, Tronson. Should we try it again?"

The guard stood behind Luke as he walked slowly up the stairs. At the top the guard opened a door and shoved Luke into the bright sunlight. Luke stood blinking. After 10 days in the hole, the sun was blinding.

Luke was marched back to the administration building. He was put through the shower again. After 10 days of barely washing, he needed it.

This time the shower went without incident. Luke left the room with the new prisoners. He was given a plastic razor and was able to cut off his 10-day beard. The razor blade was thin. Too thin, Luke thought, to use as a weapon. Or for suicide.

He was issued a simple blue prison uniform and given two thin grey wool blankets. The men were taken outside. Guards stood waiting. Each had a riot club strapped to his belt. One with a clipboard was reading off names.

"Tronson, Westgate B," he called.

Another guard walked over. "This way," he said. He motioned to a dormitory to Luke's right.

Luke walked in front of the guard until they got to the entrance. Inside, the guard on duty pushed a button on a console. A buzzer sounded. The guard accompanying Luke swung the door open and motioned Luke inside.

"OK, Tronson," he said after they got inside. "You're home."

12

It struck Luke that his dormitory sounded like a huge play school. Men were screaming and yelling all hours of the day and night. There was noise. Talking. Shouts. Men clanging the bars of their cells with cups. Crying.

Luke was glad he was on B tier. In the two tiers below him the inmates had no view. They stared out onto the fence and cold stone walls. At least Luke could see the tops of trees from his small window. And in a distance he could just make out the water of the Fraser River.

There were 32 cells on each of the four tiers; 128 cells in each block. There were five blocks. Over 600 men were doing time in Okalla.

Luke's cell, like all the others, was five feet wide and eight feet long. A bunk took up the right wall. On the other side there was a small desk. The toilet was in the corner. Inmates did what they could to make the cells theirs. They put up pictures of their girlfriends. Of their children. They put up posters or drawings. But no matter what they did, the cells remained tiny and cold.

All the doors in the cell block were electrically controlled. At 6:55 each morning they slid open. The noise of 128 heavy cell doors opening at the same time was deafening. At eight o'clock each evening they snapped shut. Every prisoner was locked into his cell for 11 hours a day.

The daily routine never changed. As soon as the doors slid open, the men trooped silently into the bathrooms to wash up. From there they went down to the mess hall for breakfast. They had exactly 30 minutes to eat. Then they returned to their cells to make their beds and clean their room. Guards inspected each cell every day. If the room was dirty or if the bed was not made well enough, a prisoner got demerit points. Enough of these and he could lose privileges. He could be banned from the TV room. He could lose his exercise period. He could even be locked up early during the prisoners' leisure time.

After inspection each prisoner would go to his work site. Prisoners worked for eight hours each day. Some worked in the laundry room. Others tended the grounds. Luke was assigned to the license plate factory. Each day he and the other prisoners stamped and packaged hundreds of sets of car license plates. Some prisoners got permission to take classes during this period. They studied to get their high school graduation. Some even took university courses.

Luke was not interested.

Recreation period was between four and five o'clock. During this time inmates could play volleyball or basketball. Some worked out in the weight room. Luke and a few others got permission to train for rodeos. They constructed a homemade chute in the corral by the cow barn. Then they rode cows.

Dinner was at 5:30. From 6:00 to 8:00 was leisure time. Prisoners played cards or watched TV. Some read. Others studied.

At eight o'clock they were back in their cells. The doors snapped shut. The prisoners were alone to write, to sleep. And to think.

Day after day rolled by without change. Even the changes of the seasons outside were muted. The prisoners could only see the sky framed by the stone walls. Just a few trees could be seen from the top tiers of cells. The men got outside only to move to their work or during their recreation time. Only the earlier nights and colder, damper days marked winter. Summer meant the sun slanted through their cell windows before the morning began.

Luke quickly realized that his dorm was controlled by the Miller-Thompson gang. They directed a large part of the drug trade in Vancouver. Just like they did in the prison. Luke got to know the gang through Max Cornell.

Soon after settling in his cell, Luke was assigned to the license plate factory. The factory was located next to the fence. They could see the big Doberman pinschers pacing back and forth behind the high chain-link fence. Occasionally they would growl and throw themselves against the mesh if an inmate looked straight at them. Their teeth were sharp and white.

Luke and other prisoners were escorted out of their cell block to the factory each morning. More prisoners joined them from other blocks. On the first day Luke saw Max come in with the group from the Northgate block. Max nodded at him and smiled.

The prisoners ate lunch in the factory. Luke had a chance to sit next to Max.

"You're Max," Luke said, extending his hand.

Max shook it firmly. He moved over on the bench so Luke could sit next to him.

"And you must be Luke," Max said smiling. "Didn't get a good look at you through that little window. But good enough."

"Max," Luke began. "I want you to know that... Well, you saved me from going nuts down there. And I..."

Max turned to his baloney sandwich and shook his head. "I don't want to hear any of that crap," he said mildly. "You would have been all right. First time in the hole is always a little scary." He gave a short laugh. " 'Course, I can hardly remember my first time."

"What were you in for this time, Max?"

"Dope. Guards caught me holding some weed. Wouldn't tell where I got it. Surprise, surprise. So they put me in the hole for 20 days."

"Twenty days!"

Max shrugged. "You get used to it."

Max looked up as a man sat down on the other side of the long table. The man wasn't tall, but Luke could see his biceps stretching the rolled sleeve of his shirt. He had jet black hair slicked back on the sides. His face was set in a scowl. He had a short white scar on his left cheek.

"Luke, let me introduce you to Mikey Miller. You're in West-gate, aren't you?"

Luke nodded.

"Mikey's in your block."

Luke extended his hand over the table. "Mikey."

The other man nodded curtly and took Luke's hand briefly.

"Miller," Max said. "Of the Miller-Thompson gang."

Luke had heard of the gang in Kamloops. In Okalla he'd already been told they were the guys to see if he wanted anything. And the guys to stay clear of.

"You're one of the Miller brothers?" Luke asked.

"That's right."

Luke gave him a tight smile. "Good to meet you."

It turned out that Mikey worked with Luke on the license plate line. Blank aluminum plates were cut out at one end. These were put in a stamper that pressed the numbers and letters into the plates. They went through rollers where they were painted white. Then they went through another set of rollers that painted the raised numbers blue.

The plates coming out of the rollers were razor sharp. Luke's job was to pull these off the line and quickly file the edges. Next to him was a huge guy named Saunders. He had a shaved head. He trimmed the paint with a tool that looked like a potato peeler. Miller stood next to Saunders. He put the plates through the glazer.

Luke minded his own business. He talked little to the men on the line with him. But from the first day he felt the tension between

Saunders and Miller. Saunders was one of the fitness freaks in the prison. He lifted huge weights and it showed. He hardly had any neck. His shirt was pulled open across his massive shoulders.

The word going around was that Saunders wanted to prove he was the toughest guy in Okalla. He wanted to show that he had no fear of the Miller-Thompson boys. Whatever he was up to, Luke didn't like it. Saunders kept up a constant chatter, insulting Miller. Taunting him.

"Hey, Miller," he'd say. "If you're so tough, why won't you get in a ring with me? Huh? Just you and me. But you're really just a little chicken shit, aren't you? Huh? Hiding behind your gang. Got your big brother outside. He fight your fights for you out there? Probably wipes your ass for you, too." He'd give a snort that was supposed to be a laugh.

It went on for hours, for days. Miller never said a word. He looked at Saunders with eyes that burned with pure hatred. But he never spoke. Luke wondered when he would explode.

One morning as they were walking into the factory, Miller grabbed Luke by the shoulder.

"I want to change jobs with you today," he said quietly.

Luke looked surprised. "Switch positions on the line?"

"Yeah."

"I don't know. Can we do that?"

"No one will notice."

Luke knew you didn't argue with the leader of the Miller-Thompson gang. He shrugged.

"OK. I guess so. But why?"

Miller's jaw was clenched. "Just need a change, that's all."

The line started, and so did Saunders.

"On my left today, eh Miller? Tired of holding my right hand? Want to hold my left for a change, you little faggot?"

The plates began to come out of the paint roller one by one. Miller picked them up and quickly dulled their edges with his file.

"Miller," Saunders continued. "You really are a disgusting coward. I mean…"

Luke wasn't sure exactly what happened next. Miller picked up a plate. Suddenly his right hand slashed savagely at Saunders and drew back. Immediately blood spurted from Saunders' throat. The big man stood there for a second, maybe two. He made a few gurgling noises. Then he collapsed on the cement floor.

When Luke looked down at Saunders, he saw blood pumping from a gaping wound in his throat. A river of blood flowed down his neck, down the front of his shirt and into a growing pool on the floor. Luke watched as Saunders' eyes glazed.

Suddenly guards ran onto the floor. The line shut down. There was yelling. One guard ran to Saunders and grabbed his wrist.

"Weak," he muttered. "Medic! Quickly!"

In moments, two orderlies from the infirmary had Saunders on a stretcher. Luke saw when they lifted him that his throat had been nearly cut to the vertebrae. Blood was everywhere.

More guards pushed the men on the line up against the wall while Saunders was removed.

Word spread through the prison like it had been broadcast on the news. Saunders was dead before he got to the infirmary.

The men on the line were questioned, of course. Miller told the warden that Saunders had slipped while picking up a sharp plate. He had accidentally cut his own throat.

Luke hadn't seen anything until the man was down. No guards had witnessed the incident. The investigation went nowhere.

The warden glared at Luke after his questioning.

"I can't make you talk, Mr. Tronson. But I am a bad enemy. I have a long memory."

Luke went back to the license plate factory the next day. It was much quieter now.

13

Luke had been in Okalla nearly a year when Bel visited him. She was the first person that had come to see him since he'd been there. He was surprised when the guard called him during the Saturday visiting hours.

"Tronson, someone to see you."

"Me?"

"Yeah, you. I don't know who the hell would want to see the likes of you either. But there's someone waiting. So get on your Sunday best and get out there."

The prisoners with visitors were escorted to the administration building. They entered a long narrow room. A row of chairs was lined up behind a long counter. On the other side sat the visitors. In between there was mesh fence that ran up to the ceiling.

When Luke entered he scanned the faces on the other side of the fence. Who was he looking for?

Then he saw Bel. She sat at the far end of the counter. She lifted a hand uncertainly when he looked in her direction. Luke smiled. For the first time in a year he felt real joy.

Luke almost ran to the chair in front of Bel. He sat down and stared through the mesh at her.

"Boy," he said. "You sure are beautiful."

Bel sniffed. "You're just horny."

"No, I mean it. You're the best thing I've seen in months."

"I guess that's a compliment," Bel laughed. "But I'm not sure considering the competition."

Luke was grinning from ear to ear. "So you came."

Bel lowered her eyes. "Yeah, I came."

"Why?"

"What kind of question is that?" Bel demanded. "Isn't it enough that I'm here?"

Luke's face was serious now. "No, it isn't. I want to know why you came. I've got to know."

Bel hesitated. "Because I can't get you out of my mind. I tried. But I can't."

Luke was smiling again. "That's what I'd hoped you say. I didn't know… what to expect. I didn't know if we still had something going. Or if I blew it."

"You blew it, for sure. But remember what I said? I don't give up easily."

They had 30 minutes. Luke found the words tumbling out. He had so much to say. Finally the guard announced that visiting time was over. Luke put his left hand against the metal mesh of the fence. Bel raised her right hand to his. Luke felt the heat from her hand.

"I'm up for parole in three months," he said. "Can you wait?"

Bel dropped her hand and picked up her purse off the counter.

"I'm not going anywhere."

She stood up and turned to leave. Luke kept sitting, staring through the mesh at her. At the door she turned.

"Love you," she whispered. Then she was gone.

Luke was assigned a parole officer to help him prepare for his parole hearing. Luke wasn't eligible until he had served 18 months of his sentence. But he knew it could take months to get a hearing. So Luke had put his application for a hearing in soon after his first year was up.

One day he was called off the line. He was escorted to a small room in the administration building. A sign over the door read "Counselling."

Inside there was a large grey table with a chair on either side. A middle-aged woman sat in one. She looked up at Luke as he entered. She had short grey hair. There were frown lines around her lips. She didn't laugh a lot, Luke decided. But that didn't matter when he looked into her eyes. They were dark and deep. Luke saw pain in them. Toughness. And there was something else. Compassion.

Luke stood by the door. The woman motioned to the other chair.

"Come in, Mr. Tronson. Please sit down," she said.

Luke walked over and pulled out the chair. He leaned backwards on the two back legs.

"Are you a counsellor?" he asked. "I didn't even know they had counsellors here."

The woman looked down at papers on the desk. She gave a short laugh.

"Oh, yeah. They've got a counsellor. One for 600 men. That ought to straighten you out, eh?"

"You know one thing I never understood?"

"What's that, Mr. Tronson?"

"Well, they say they send people to jail to reform them. But that's not right." Luke hesitated. "If they really want to reform people, jail isn't the place to send them. I mean, what do I learn here? How to pull off better robberies. And get away with it. I mean it's great if you want to stay in the criminal field. You make terrific contacts—gangs, bikers, dope pushers." Luke shook his head. "If you want to learn about crime, go to jail."

The woman was still looking at her papers. She sighed wearily. "Very well put, Mr. Tronson. Now if we could just convince some of our citizens of that. Maybe we could create a system that made people more human rather than less human."

She looked up at Luke. Her mouth turned down at the corners grimly. She extended her hand across the table.

"I'm Paula Woods."

Luke leaned forward and took her hand. He stood up slightly. "Pleased to meet you."

Paula gave Luke a tiny smile. "Well, aren't we gallant."

Luke sat back, embarrassed.

"Anyway, Mr. Tronson, to answer your question. No, I am not a counsellor. I am the parole officer assigned to your case. My job is to prepare with you your hearing for the parole board. That may be some months away. But we need to start now." She paused, looking at Luke with those deep, dark eyes.

"I'm not a counsellor, Mr. Tronson, but I do need to know about your past. Frankly, your record since you have been in jail is not great." She frowned even deeper. "We're not going to get you out of here unless we can show some background. And you stay out of any more trouble."

Luke shifted uncomfortably in his chair. "I don't really like to talk about my past. My family."

Paula's face remained grim and set. "And I really don't want to hear about it, Mr. Tronson. But we are going to have to show that your past was a factor in your problems. Is that true?"

"Hell, I don't know."

"Well, let's start by talking a little about growing up. Was your father a kind man?"

Luke snorted. "Not that I ever saw. He was big, rough, and an alcoholic. He beat me nearly every day. He especially liked to use an old razor strap. It was a heavy piece of leather three inches wide. When I got a whipping with that it felt like he was pulling the meat right off of me."

"I see. And what about your mother?"

"My mom tried to protect me. She knew I was wild. Different from my younger brothers and sisters. There were eight of us by the time I left at 13. Damn near one a year. She'd say, 'You gotta do things this way or your dad will get mad.' But it didn't matter if I did. He'd get mad at me anyway. I just figured he had something in for me. I was the black sheep of the family."

Paula was jotting notes in a small notebook. "And how did all this make you feel?"

Luke thought for a minute. "I kind of got it in my mind that it didn't matter what you did. You just did things your way. If you got in trouble for it, you just took it."

"How about those brothers and sisters?" Paula asked.

Luke ran his hand through his hair.

"Listen, lady, Paula. You've got to understand. I grew up in a rough family. I was always being compared to the others. And I was never good enough. For my dad at least. If I couldn't keep up—in school or in fights or whatever—he would take me out and beat the piss out of me. That's the way he said I'd learn."

Paula put down her pen. Her eyes looked softer than before.

"I guess he was right," she said.

"How's that?"

"You learned. You learned really well."

14

Paula met with Luke each week for several months. Slowly his story unfolded. Luke was surprised to hear it himself. Sometimes he was angry. Sometimes he would find tears welling in his eyes. Like when he described how his mother started to drink. And how lonely he felt without her.

Paula was the first person Luke had ever talked to about his past. And she was the first person to help him see that he needed to get beyond it.

During one session Luke had described how his father began beating his mother. And how he would try to stop him. As he spoke the rage rose in him like a flame.

"And when I grabbed him, he'd turn on me." Luke's fist slammed the top of the desk. "And he'd beat me until my face was bloody." His voice rose until he was screaming hoarsely. "My mother would be crying and trying to stop him. The other kids would be hiding. And he would be howling at me." Luke swept Paula's coffee mug off the table. It smashed on the brown tile. Luke stood up and paced back and forth.

Paula was quiet for some time. Then she got up and picked up the pieces of the mug. She put them in a wastebasket. Then she sat down again. Luke was still pacing angrily.

"Luke," she said at last. "You're going to have to get a handle on your anger."

Luke glared at her.

"This is not therapy," she went on. "But you could use some. And I hope you get it. Let me just say one thing. I am not going through this to let you off the hook. The fact that you were abused does not give you permission to rob, steal and hurt people. Many others with backgrounds as bad or worse than yours have made other choices."

Luke had his hands curled around the back of the chair. His fingers dug into the cloth.

"I am putting together information for a parole hearing. You need to start putting things together for your life. You've had it rough. You have lots of reasons to feel angry. But you have also made some awfully bad choices. You have got to start making better ones. Or else you're going to wallow in the past. Is that where you want to be?"

Luke leaned on the chair and stared at the seat. Paula closed her notebook and got ready to leave.

"You'd better get over the past and get on with your future. If you don't, you're going to be here or in another jail for the rest of your life. Is that what you want?" She walked to the door and pushed a buzzer. "Think about it."

Bel visited him once or twice a month. She was still waitressing.

It was hard for her to get away. And her old Camaro was acting up. It was a five hour drive from Vernon. But Luke knew she tried. And he looked forward to her visits so much it hurt.

Bel was a future. Without her, there was only a blank. And sometimes Luke's need for her scared Bel.

"Luke," she said during one visit. "I'm no answer. I have my own problems. I can't be everything to you. It's not fair. I can't be your lover, friend, mother and counsellor. You need to find those in other people too."

Luke knew he was pushing her. Asking too much. But he needed her, desperately.

"I'm sorry," he said to her. "I'm trying. But Bel," he added. "Don't give up on me. OK?"

Bel smiled. "I won't."

Luke also looked forward to his sessions with Paula. At one meeting she was actually smiling. "Luke, good news," she said. "Your parole hearing is scheduled for next month."

Luke had been in Okalla for 16 months. Parole offered him hope. A chance to get out. To be with Bel. To win the Provincials. To make a life.

Luke was also scared. "Will I get it?"

"I've got to be honest with you. I really don't know. We'll give it our best shot."

The parole hearing was held in another room of the administration building. Luke was escorted in by a guard. He stood by the door. Luke sat at a table next to Paula.

In front of them was a long table. Four people sat at the table facing Luke. Luke was startled to see the warden sitting at the far end.

Luke leaned over to Paula. "What's he doing here?" he whispered.

Paula shuffled her notes. "It's not good. He has asked to intervene."

"What's that mean?"

"He's got something to say about your parole."

Luke groaned.

The hearing was quite informal. First the chairman reviewed Luke's conviction record. There were 12 charges, nine convictions. Armed robbery, assault, breaking and entering, assault… Luke cringed as each one was read out.

Then it was Paula's turn. She gave some background on Luke. She spoke about his past. His abusive home. That he left home at 13. That he had never broken into a home. He had never hurt anyone during a break in.

Then she spoke about how she had seen Luke grow. How he had become more willing to look at his past. And to plan a future.

Luke couldn't tell how this was going down with the panel. After Paula was finished the panel members asked Luke questions.

"Mr. Tronson," the chairman asked. "What is your plan for the future?"

Paula had coached him for this one. "I am trained as a cook. I intend to get a job in a restaurant. I have a girlfriend. We hope to be married."

Paula had told him to say just enough. Not to elaborate too much. But be definite. Be positive.

A woman in a blue suit spoke next. "And what will be different this time, Mr. Tronson? Why won't you land in the courts again?"

Luke wasn't sure himself. "Well, I'll have a job. A wife. I'll ride rodeo."

Another woman spoke up. "It sounds like you're looking for everyone else to keep you straight. What about you?"

Luke hesitated. Paula sensed his confusion.

"Mr. Tronson is anxious to get counselling," Paula said. "He is aware that he needs to continue to grow."

"Is that true, Mr. Tronson?" the woman asked.

"Yes, ma'am," Luke answered. "I'll get into counselling as soon as I get out. I don't want to end up back here. Ever."

The questions were tough, but Luke got through them. He thought he was making a good impression. The woman in the blue suit even smiled at him. He had just told her that his ambition was to win the Provincial bull riding championship buckle.

"I hope you do," she said.

After an hour the chairman looked up and down the table.

"Is that about it? Any other questions?" he asked.

There were a few seconds of silence.

"I'm afraid I have a few comments I'd like to provide." The warden spoke from the end of the table. The four board members turned to the warden.

"Oh, no," Luke said quietly.

"Mr. Tronson makes a good case for himself. But I have to make a few unpleasant points." The warden never looked at Luke. "Within one hour of arriving at this prison Mr. Tronson was in a fight. Several months later there was a death. Mr. Tronson was not a suspect. But he would not tell us what happened. We have reason to feel that he was covering up a murder."

Luke could see the faces of the board. They had suddenly become set and stern.

"In my opinion Mr. Tronson is trouble. His history suggests it. His behaviour here proves it. I cannot support his application for parole."

Luke felt the old anger rise in him. He started to open his mouth. Paula dug an elbow in his side. He clenched his teeth and glared at the warden.

There was another silence. This one was longer.

"I see," the chairman said at last. "Well, we have enough to go on I believe. You will all be informed of our decision within the week."

And then it was over.

Five days later Luke was called to the counselling room. Paula sat glumly in her chair. Luke knew instantly that he had been turned down. He turned to the closed door and kicked it. "Damn!" he yelled. "They turned me down." Luke smashed the door with his fist. He hit it again. Blood started to ooze from his knuckles. "God *damn* it!"

Paula waited quietly. When Luke had calmed down, she pointed to the chair.

"Sit down, Luke." Luke stalked over to the chair and slammed himself into it. "You're right. They turned you down."

"It was that god damned warden!" Luke hissed.

"No, Luke," Paula said. "It was you. You got into the fight. Not the warden."

Luke sulked in the chair.

"Are you ready to listen?"

Luke didn't say anything. He nodded slightly.

"You can get another hearing in three months."

"A lot of good that will do," Luke snarled. "The warden will just speak against it again. I don't have a chance."

"You do if you can prove that you've done something. That you've changed."

"And how the hell can I do that in here?" Luke yelled. "I didn't even know they *had* a counsellor here till you told me."

"Not here."

Luke looked at her, puzzled. "What are you talking about? This is where I am and I'm obviously not getting out."

"Not if you volunteer for a wilderness camp."

"A wilderness camp? What's that? You mean I go live in a tent?"

Paula smiled a little. "It's not quite that bad. But it isn't easy. You'll be tested. Physically and mentally. They'll run you. Make you work. You'll climb cliffs. Jump off platforms. That kind of thing. You'll learn to work with others. And you'll have a counsellor assigned to you."

"What good would all that do?"

"Listen," Paula said fiercely. "Who do you think you are? So you've had it rough. That's too bad! Get over it. And here's a chance to do it!"

Luke sat uncertainly. "How do you know I can get in?"

"When I got the word about your parole I went to the warden. I convinced him. He said he'd give it a chance. But he didn't think it would work."

"He's probably right!" Luke exploded. "I'm just a low life crook like they say I am! Why should I bother?"

Paula looked evenly at him. Now her eyes were cool, steady.

"If you really believe that then stay here. Rot. Prove the warden right. Don't do anything to change. You'll get out eventually. But you'll be back." She paused.

"It's your decision, your choice." She sat back heavily in her chair. "Make the right one."

15

The Ginsberg Lake Wilderness Camp was somewhere north of Pemberton. At least Luke thought the van headed north after they passed through the town. All he knew for certain was that there wasn't much around. First the pavement ended. Then the dirt road became rutted. They rumbled over rough logging bridges. Mountains reared on either side. They seemed to be going up steadily.

Finally the van pulled into a wide spot by a large lake. There seemed to be a sandy landing below them. The driver turned off the engine. One guard walked to the back of the van and opened the door. The other stood with a riot gun by the front door. The four prisoners inside got out. They looked around uncertainly. They couldn't see cabins or a trail. Only the road showed people had ever been there. On the far side of the lake dark trees covered steep mountain sides.

"Where the hell are we?" Saul Stevens asked.

"This, gentlemen, is Goode Lake," said the guard that opened the door.

"Great," Saul replied. "But what does that have to do with us?"

Luke thought he saw a small boat approaching from the far shore.

"Be patient, gentlemen," the guard replied. "You'll be in your new home soon enough. And I daresay after a few days you may wish you were back here."

By this time the boat was clearly visible. They could hear its faint droning across the water. Luke could make out two figures.

Ten minutes later the boat landed on the sandy stretch below them. Luke heard the keel grind along the gravel as the boat glided into shore. Two men got out. They were dressed in jeans and flannel shirts. One wore a red nylon windbreaker. They walked up from the boat to the van.

The man in the red windbreaker looked them over one by one. Finally he spoke.

"Gentlemen. Welcome to Ginsberg Lake Wilderness Camp. My name is Bryan Hodges. I am the camp coordinator. Please grab your packs out of the van and follow me to the boat."

The men did as they were told. As Luke shouldered his pack he hoped he wouldn't have to walk far. The pack must have weighed 45 pounds. They followed Bryan back down the slope to the boat. It was a large aluminum craft with high sides. It had an inboard engine that roared into life as Bryan turned a key. The four prisoners threw their packs into the boat and climbed aboard. They sat on cold aluminum benches in the middle of the boat.

The other man had said nothing. He was a huge bear of a man.

His shaggy black hair and beard hung down on his red and black checked flannel shirt. He sat by himself in the back of the boat.

Bryan backed the boat out into the lake and pushed the throttle forward. They surged across the water toward the other side of Goode Lake.

The day was overcast and chilly. The wind in the open boat cut through their prison shirts like a knife. They were glad to see the rocky shore approaching. They could make out a small dock sticking out from the wooded shoreline.

At last the boat pulled up beside the dock. Bryan jumped out and tied a line to a ring set in the logs of the dock. The other man climbed out and did the same in the rear. Luke and the other men picked up their gear and clambered onto the dock.

"OK," Bryan said to them. "We're about a half hour from the camp. It's located by Ginsberg Lake in a valley west of here. But first you are going to have to get above that ridge." Bryan pointed almost straight up. Luke could see only a steep slope. It looked more like a cliff. A few trees managed to hang on to its sheer sides.

"There's a trail," Bryan said, pointing vaguely ahead with his chin. Great, Luke thought. I figured we were going to have to do it with ropes.

"So get your packs on," Bryan continued. "And I've got something else I need you to carry up."

He walked down the log dock. He stood by a pile of cedar blocks. "Over here!" he yelled.

The four men, followed by the bear, shouldered their packs. They walked to the shore where Bryan was standing. He pointed to the pile of cedar blocks. They were about two feet across. Luke figured they were almost that long.

"We're reshaking the main hall," Bryan said. "We need to move these blocks up to the camp. I want you each to carry one up to the top of the ridge."

"Up there?" squeaked Saul. "Man, I'll be dead before I get halfway."

"Then the rest of the men will have to carry your body back down." Bryan said mildly. Luke and the rest of the men looked at each other uneasily. What had they gotten themselves into?

"And then I want you to drop your packs and come down for another." Bryan paused. "Got it? All right, move."

Luke grabbed one of the blocks. It must have weighed 30 pounds. His pack was so heavy he was afraid he wasn't going to be able to stand up. But he did. He staggered up the narrow path in front of him.

The path wound steadily upward. In most places they couldn't go straight up. Switchbacks cut across the face of the steep slope. They struggled on. Step by painful step. Sweat poured from Luke until he was drenched. Once he stumbled and landed on his block. He grunted and tried to get his breath. From the rear he heard Bryan.

"Move it along up there! You're holding us all up!"

Luke fought to his feet and lurched upward.

After what seemed like hours Luke stumbled over the edge of the ridge. The trail ran straight and level into the trees. Luke collapsed, gasping for air. His breath rasped in and out. Behind him he heard the other men stagger into the clearing. He looked up as Bryan bounced over the top of the trail. He was carrying the largest block of all. Luke noticed he wasn't even sweating. Right after him came the bear. He was carrying two blocks.

"OK. Not bad. Now drop your packs and head back down for another block."

"I can't, man! Seriously!" Saul groaned. "I'm dead!"

"Dead men don't talk, Mr. Stevens," Bryan replied evenly. "Down you go. All of you."

Luke lurched to his feet and slipped the straps off his shoulders. He felt the cool breeze on the soaked back of his shirt.

"Let's go," Luke said quietly.

Pat John stood up. He brushed his long black hair back. He took off his pack. Then Mike Sanchez joined them.

Saul looked up from the ground. He groaned and lay flat on the ground.

"I can't make it," he gasped. "But don't let me slow you down. You men go on without me." His voice dwindled to a whisper. He pretended to faint.

Pat and Mike laughed. Bryan shook his head.

"You'll be great in the role-plays, Stevens" he said.

Saul opened one eye and looked up. "Didn't work, eh?"

He sprang to his feet and pulled off his pack. "Last one down's a wimp."

He ran over the edge of the ridge. The others looked at one another. Then they scrambled after him.

After they had brought up another block, Bryan led them to the camp. It was about a kilometre from the ridge. Mercifully, the trail was pretty level. Still, they were exhausted when they stumbled over a rise into a large clearing. The rocky ground sloped away to the shore of a lake. Luke figured the lake was two kilometres long. The water was brilliant blue. To their right a mountain peak rose out of the lake. On their left, below them, several small cabins were scattered in the trees. A larger building stood in the middle. In front of it there were ropes strung between trees.

Bryan paused at the edge of the clearing. The silent bear came up behind.

"This is Ginsberg Lake Camp, gentlemen," Bryan said. He paused. The men's eyes swept across the lake and up to the mountain peak above it.

"I hope each of you finds something important here."

The prisoners looked up at him. He looked each of them straight in the eyes.

"Now, let's get you settled in."

He led the way down the slope to the cabins. Luke counted eight of them. They were small, about eight feet by 10. Each was made of logs with a cedar shake roof. A simple wood door led into each cabin. There were no locks on the doors.

Bryan stopped by a cabin with the number "4" on it. They stepped in. It was almost bare inside. Against two walls there were a pair of bunks. A simple table and a single chair sat under the window in the far wall.

"This will be your men's cabin for the next three months. Keep it clean. Drop your packs inside. The other men and counsellors are out in the bush right now. They will be back in about an hour. Come over to the dining hall when you hear the bell ring. You'll be introduced to your counsellors."

"Bryan," Saul said. "Can I call you Bryan?"

"That's my name."

"Bryan, this isn't some sort of secret concentration camp where they murder prisoners, is it? I mean, if it is let's get it over now. Just shoot me. Don't torture me first."

Bryan's eyes twinkled. "Most men get out alive, Saul."

Saul nodded. "That's reassuring. Thanks, Bryan."

16

For the first week Luke was sure Saul had it right. They *were* being tortured. A huge bell outside the main building was rung exactly at 6:30 each morning. They scuttled from their beds to the lake front. Then they stripped and plunged into the icy water. Luke had never been so cold.

They dashed screaming back to their cabins. They dried and pulled on sweat suits. They filed into the main building where they ate breakfast. Luke had never eaten granola in his life. Now he ate it every morning.

They followed this with a five-kilometre run around the lake. Then there were exercises. Set after set of push-ups. Sit-ups. Arm curls with weights.

After that the counsellors put them through the "high opportunities." They looked like obstacles to Luke. But the counsellors insisted on calling them "high ops."

"You've got to stop thinking of things as obstacles," explained Bob. Bob was one of the counsellors. "Every experience is an opportunity. An opportunity to grow. Look on these challenges as an opportunity to grow."

"Yeah," muttered Saul. "Or an opportunity to die."

Some of the "high ops" involved walking across ropes strung between trees. The ropes were 20 feet off the ground. Each man had on a safety harness. But it was still scary. Another challenge was walking across a two-inch beam. The only problem was it was 20 feet long and 25 feet off the ground.

Luke had figured that this would be easy for him. He was used to danger. Used to keeping his balance. And most of the challenges weren't too bad. But then he came up on the trapeze.

The trapeze challenge was truly terrifying for Luke. He was cocky at first. He had seen other men climb 30 feet up the ladder on the side of the thick post. At the top of the post was a small platform. It was about two feet square. The men stood on the platform and clicked their safety line onto a rope above them. Five feet in front hung a trapeze. From the swaying platform they jumped for the trapeze. They grabbed it with both hands. Then they swung, 30 feet above the ground. Finally they were lowered down by one of the counsellors.

On the third day Luke's group was scheduled for the trapeze. Pat went first. He made the jump and swung to the ground. He was smiling.

Then Mike climbed up. He stood on the swaying platform. He looked scared. He hesitated.

"You can do it!" Bob shouted from below. "Take a risk! Find your power!" Other men called encouragement.

Mike jumped. His hands hit the bar of the trapeze. His right hand caught. But his left hand missed. He dangled for a second from one hand. Then he slipped.

The safety rope caught him just a few feet after his fall. When he came down Mike was shaking his head.

"Not quite. I'll get it next time."

Saul was standing in front of Luke. "Next time," he said. "Man, I'm worried about *this* time. Listen Luke, I know I've called you a bow-legged little bugger. But don't make me go first. Please." Saul got on his knees and pretended to beg.

Luke grinned. "Get up, you chicken. I'll show you how to do it."

So Luke started up the ladder. About halfway up, the pole began to sway. Felt kind of like a bull, he thought. But then he looked down. Bulls weren't 20 feet off the ground.

He came to the platform. He had to climb over the edge. He raised himself above the side. His feet were still on the ladder rungs. The pole swayed. Luke looked down again. He thought he was going to pass out. He froze.

"OK, Luke. Take it easy." It was Bob, calling from below. "Don't look down. Grab the sides and pull yourself up. You can do it."

"Or if you can't, all you'll do is fall down and be paralyzed for life," Saul called out helpfully.

Luke reached out and grabbed the plywood edges. He eased himself onto the platform. Then he had to stand up.

It took him minutes. He inched up on the swaying square of wood. Men were shouting encouragement below. Luke never looked down. Finally he was standing almost straight. He managed to snap his safety line. Ahead of him was the three-foot bar. It looked like it was a mile away.

Luke's heart was racing. Adrenaline pumped through him. It was just like sitting on a bull. But scarier. Then he heard nothing. The shouts of the men vanished. He focussed on the bar. He felt his legs straighten. He leapt for the bar.

The bar struck Luke on the wrists. He started to fall. Then his fingers tightened around the wood trapeze. He held on. He swung slowly, high in the air.

Sound returned. He heard men cheering below him. He looked down.

He shouldn't have. As soon as he saw the ground swinging between his feet, his gut clenched. He held on with all his might.

"Good work," Bob yelled from the ground. "But now you have to let go. We'll lower you down."

Letting go was the second hardest thing Luke had ever done. He squeezed his eyes shut and loosened his grip. He slipped off the bar and found himself floating gently to earth. He sighed thankfully when his shoes hit the dirt.

Bob came over smiling. He unhitched him from the safety harness.

"Congratulations," he said. Luke saw that he meant it. "You've looked fear square in the eye. And you overcame it."

"Ha," called Saul. "I thought I was going to have to come there and pry your fingers loose. Man, you looked like you had Crazy Glue on your hands!"

"Thank you for those kind words," Luke said. He smiled evilly. "Now it's your turn."

Besides the "high ops," there were "low ops." These were at least on the ground. But they required team work. They were like group puzzles.

For one, a group of six men had to get from one four-foot square of wood to another. It was eight feet away. The problem was they couldn't step in between. They were told to imagine that it was a river filled with crocodiles. All they had to get to the other side was a rope that hung between the two squares. And they had to take a five-gallon bucket of water with them.

First they had to figure out how to get the rope. Then they tried to decide who should swing over first. The first man had to send the rope back. More and more men packed the small space. They had to catch each other. They had to hold each other to keep from falling into the "river." And how were they going to get the bucket across without spilling the water? Saul had the idea of tying the handle to the rope and the last man—him—swinging it across to the others. Of course he pushed it so hard it sloshed over the other five. When Saul got across, Mike and Luke held him. Pat poured the rest of the water over his head.

Another "low op" looked like a giant spider web made of ropes. A group of eight men had to get through the web without touching it. And they couldn't use the same hole twice. They had to lift from both sides. They had to be patient. They had to work together.

And after the challenges there was more running. And more exercises. And then there were the counsellors.

17

There was one counsellor for every four inmates. Right after breakfast, the counsellors met with each of their clients. They'd ask each man how he was doing. What he was thinking about. What he was feeling. How the course was going. In the evening after supper, the counsellors would check in again.

During the day the men could ask to speak to a counsellor at any time. Sometimes they would sit and talk in the main building. Often they would walk along the lake.

David was Luke's counsellor. He was a little older than Luke. Not a big guy, but wiry. He had long blond hair he usually wore in a pony tail. He was a nationally-known mountaineer. And over time, he became Luke's friend.

Once they were walking on the trail around the lake. Luke asked David if he could have a few minutes. They walked single file along the rolling trail. Occasionally they could see trout in the crystal clear water. David walked ahead.

"So how are you making out, Luke?" David asked.

Luke watched his feet. "I don't know. I feel really confused."

"About your future?"

"Oh, man, my future. My past. What I want."

The path widened. David dropped back to walk side-by-side. He picked up a few rocks and skipped them across the still surface of the lake. They walked in silence for a long time.

"I don't know where I'm going. What's important. You know what I mean?"

They walked quietly for a few more minutes. Then David glanced at Luke.

"OK, let me ask you this. What do you want more than anything else in the world? Be specific."

Luke thought as they climbed a low hill. "The buckle, I guess. The provincial bull riding championship."

David nodded. "OK, and what would that give you?"

"I just told you," Luke said shortly. "The buckle."

"But the buckle is just a buckle. What would that buckle represent?"

Luke shoved his hands into the pockets of his jeans.

"I don't know," he mumbled. "That I was the best. It would mean respect."

"Ah, so it's respect you want."

"Well, sure. Doesn't everyone?"

"Uh huh," David nodded. "I think so. But there's different ways of getting it. Who do you want respect from?"

Luke shrugged. "People. I don't know."

"Anyone in particular?"

Now Luke slowed down. He stopped at a rocky point. He

looked out over the lake. To his left, the sharp peak of the mountain was white against the blue sky.

"My dad, I guess," Luke said finally. "He hated me. I never did anything right. Nothing was good enough for him."

"So you want respect from your father. He's dead, right?" Luke nodded. "So it's not likely you're going to get much respect from him now, eh?"

Luke looked up. He felt anger. But David's eyes were clear. Sincere.

Luke shrugged again. "I guess not."

"So maybe he couldn't show you respect. Love. Maybe *he* was hurt, damaged. Not you."

"Yeah," Luke agreed. "Maybe."

"And now the point is that you don't need his respect. Can't get it anyway. So whose respect do you want now?"

"I don't know. Bel's. People's."

"And how are you going to get it?" They started walking again. "Think about it, Luke. I'm not sure a belt buckle is going to do it."

In the afternoons there were group sessions. Sometimes all 32 men and the eight counsellors would meet. More often eight or 16 would meet. Each session had a theme.

They learned about assertiveness. Whole days were spent on developing listening skills. They were drilled on problem solving techniques. They talked about stress: how to talk to yourself to reduce stress. Then they learned relaxation techniques. They practiced breathing exercises. Muscle relaxation exercises. And meditation.

Luke was sitting down on the floor. His legs were crossed and his eyes were closed. He was saying "Relax" to himself. Then he began to giggle. He opened his eyes. David walked over to him. He was smiling slightly.

"Embarrassed?" he asked.

"Nah," Luke whispered. "I just never thought I'd be sitting on a floor with my eyes closed with 30 cons. Saying 'Relax.' "

"Know what you mean," David said. "It makes me nervous sometimes too."

And then there were the anger workshops.

Those were led by Ramon. Ramon was the big bear that had met Luke at the boat. Luke had gotten to like Ramon. He wasn't quiet exactly. He was—Luke wasn't quite sure of the word— serene, maybe. Calm. And when he talked about anger, Luke listened.

Luke quit seeing anger as a bad emotion and that it was OK to feel angry sometimes. He began to realize that there was a difference between feeling angry and acting on it. And that letting anger out didn't get rid of it.

"If that were the case," Ramon pointed out, "the angriest people would have the least anger. Has that been your experience? Anger can become a habit."

But the hardest idea was that he chose his anger.

"You see," Ramon said. "Nothing or no one makes you angry. We choose to respond with anger. We create it."

"Come on," Luke burst out. "That's crap. People push me around, they piss me off. They put me down, that makes me mad!"

"Whoa," Ramon replied. "I'm not saying that you shouldn't get angry sometimes. That might be the right response. It might help you take action to right a wrong. But the fact is you choose to respond with anger."

"Oh, man," Saul called out. "You don't know my girlfriend."

"OK, let me give you an example. You walk by a friend's house and he sticks his head out. He screams at you. He calls you a bastard. A slimy creep. How do you feel?"

"I'm pissed, man," Pat John volunteered. "I'll go smack his face."

"OK," Ramon continued. "Now you're walking by a mental institution. The same friend leans out and yells the same stuff. How do feel now?"

"Well, I feel sorry for the guy," Pat said.

"You don't feel angry?"

"No, it's different. The guy's sick."

"But the same event took place. He called you names. You see, the difference is that you took it differently. You interpreted it differently. So you reacted differently. You talk to yourself all the time. *You* decide how you are going to respond. Not the situation."

They did a written anger inventory. They had to indicate how angry they would get in different situations. Luke's score was almost off the scale. The key said, "You are a true anger champion. Your anger may often get out of control. This may lead to outbursts that get you into trouble."

Yeah, no kidding, thought Luke.

They role-played situations where they had gotten angry. In one, Luke was asked to describe a situation where anger had gotten him into trouble. Luke thought a minute.

"Jobs," he said. "A guy bosses me around, I explode."

"OK," Ramon said. "Let's act it out. I'm your boss. Where?"

"A restaurant."

"OK, I'm your boss at a restaurant. I'm going to give you a hard time. What are you going to do?"

"Talk to myself."

"That'll be a dull conversation," Saul said from the group. Ramon frowned at him.

They did it. Luke stood by a table pretending to cut up vegetables. Ramon started in on him.

"Hey, quit loafing! I wanted that stuff half an hour ago. Come on, we've got customers waiting. What's the hold up?"

It was a role-play, but Luke felt the anger rising as if it were real. Then he talked to himself: I'm getting angry. But as long as I keep cool, I am in charge here. I'm getting better at these situations all the time. Take a few deep breaths. Time to relax and slow things down. I'm not going to take this personally. I know I can manage this situation.

And it worked. Ramon kept badgering, and Luke felt himself calm down.

At the end, Ramon grinned. "How do you feel?"

"A little uptight, but OK. OK. I got through it. Yeah, I'm getting better."

And he was. His body was as hard as wood. And inside he was feeling more centred than ever before. More confident.

At last, the three months were up. There was a graduation. All the men sat outside in a circle. The men who were leaving stood up and spoke about what they had learned. What their hopes were for the future. Their fears.

Luke figured he could do that, no problem. But when it was his time things turned out differently. He looked at the faces of his counsellors. They were all smiling encouragement. Then he looked at the men who had gone through so much with him. And tears began to well in his eyes. They rolled down his cheeks. His throat closed. There was silence.

"Oh, man," Saul finally called out. "Let's go to the next guy. This one's going to take all day."

Luke laughed with the other men. And then he spoke.

"I haven't got a lot to say," he managed. "I just want to thank all of you for being here. For being friends. I've never had this many friends before. Without you I'd still be the angry little geek I was when I came here." Luke paused to wipe his nose.

"Well, you're still a little geek," Saul called out.

"And in closing," Luke said. "I sincerely hope Saul falls out of the boat on the way back and drowns."

18

Luke's second parole hearing was held just a few days after his return to Okalla. Paula had made the arrangements while he was away. Now they sat together. They looked at six people across from them. The chairperson was the woman who had worn the blue suit during Luke's first hearing. The warden sat at the end again.

The hearing followed the lines of the first. But this time after the woman reviewed Luke's convictions, she paused.

"Mr. Tronson," she said. "I understand that you have just completed three months in a wilderness camp."

"Yes ma'am," Luke responded.

"Would you care to tell us how things have changed. Why you are now more ready to rejoin society than at the time of your last hearing?"

Luke hesitated. He looked at Paula. Her set lips were closed. She nodded at him. Luke stood up.

"Three months ago you asked me a question," he began. "You said that I was looking for everyone else to keep me straight. You said, 'What about you?' " Luke placed his hands on the table. He leaned toward the panel.

"And you were right. All my life I have been blaming others. I felt that I owed nobody anything. That I could do whatever I wanted. No matter who I hurt.

"Oh, I was ready to pay the penalty. But that was part of it. No one cared about me. I cared about no one. They were out to get me. I had to get them first. But those months at Ginsberg Lake showed me another side. People cared about me. And I cared about them."

Luke felt his throat start to close. He swallowed.

"And I learned that I have to do three things. I have to recognize the problems I have. These are anger, mainly. But also feeling bad about myself. Feeling cut off from everyone. And then I have to take responsibility for those. And then..." Luke paused and looked each member of the panel in the eyes. Then he looked at the warden. "And then I have to work toward solving them. With support I think I can do that now."

Luke looked at each of them again. Then he sat down. There was silence in the room.

There were a few more questions. And then the chairperson turned to the warden.

"Do you have any comments, Warden?" she asked.

Luke felt Paula hold her breath. He looked down at the table. The silence stretched on for several seconds.

"No," the warden said finally. "I have nothing to add."

Luke heard Paula exhale quietly.

The chairperson smiled at Luke. "We'll notify you within a few days."

Bel was waiting for him in the parking lot outside of the gates. Paula was there to meet him as well. He felt the sun on his back. He heard the traffic on the highway in front of him. Luke heard the heavy gates swing shut behind. He didn't look back. He ran to Bel. She was standing by the open door of her old blue Camaro. He grabbed her fiercely.

"Easy," she said kissing him. "You'll break my back."

Paula walked over. "Congratulations, Luke," she said. Luke thought there was a hint of a smile on her lips. "Stay clean. Meet your parole restrictions. And…" She looked at Bel. "And good luck."

She held out her hand. Luke took it. Then he hugged her around the neck.

"Thanks," he said, still hugging her. "Thanks for everything."

Paula shook her head. "I didn't do anything. Just my job. You did the work."

Luke let her go and stood back. Paula was dabbing her eyes.

"Get out of here now," she said. "And for God's sake, don't ever come back."

The drive to Vernon had been like a dream for Luke. The colours were brilliant. He lowered the window and stuck his head out. He opened his mouth and sucked in great lungfuls of air. He hugged Bel until she pushed him away playfully.

"Luke!" she said. "Not now. I'm driving."

Finally they drove into downtown Vernon. Luke noticed businesses he'd broken into. But he also saw the faces of people on the street. There were happy faces. And sad ones. But they were people, with lives and fears. And hopes. Just like me, Luke thought.

They wound through town. They pulled into the parking lot by Bel's apartment. Luke lugged in his suitcase. Bel made coffee. She poured some for Luke. They sat quietly at Bel's kitchen table. Luke stared out the window. Bel reached over and took his hand.

"Let's move to the bedroom," she said.

Luke hesitated. He laughed a little and looked down at his coffee cup.

"I'm nervous as hell," he said. "I haven't been with a woman in nearly two years."

Bel squeezed his hand.

"I'm not going to lie to you, Luke. I was with a guy for a while. A few months after you left. I was mad at you. Confused."

Luke looked up. His eyes were wide.

"What happened?"

Bel shrugged and smiled. "Not much. I realized he wasn't you. And you were who I wanted." She waggled her head. "After a few months I told him goodbye. That was it."

Luke squeezed her hand now.

"Thanks," he said. "Thanks for telling me."

"Look at me, Luke." Luke looked up into her deep brown eyes. "I love you." She stood and pulled him up from the table. She pulled him by the hand toward the bedroom. She looked back over her shoulder.

"I'll be gentle," she said.

"So you'll come with me? Promise?" Luke was excited. He had been bull riding all season. He was number three in the province. And the provincial championships were the next weekend.

Bel smiled. "Yeah, I'll come with you. If it means so much to you."

"Bel, you don't know," Luke said. "No one has ever come see me ride. Never. Not one of my brothers. No one."

"There's Harvey."

"He doesn't count. He's a rider."

"Well what about Saul? He came all the way up from Burnaby." Luke smiled at the memory.

"He came up to see us. He just came to the rodeo because there was nothing else to do. Besides, all he did was drink beer and pick up women. He didn't see me ride one bull."

"Well, it's the thought that counts," Bel said.

"So if you'll come, boy… That would be great!"

"OK, OK," Bel laughed. "I said I'd come."

"I spoke to Manny. He'll give me time off." Manny owned the Piccolo Inn. Luke had worked there as a cook for almost a year since he had gotten out of jail. "And I can get my school work done at night." Luke was taking upgrading at the local college.

"Yeah, right. I'll believe that when I see it," Bel said.

"We can stay in the camper."

"That'll be a treat."

Luke was so excited he was hopping from foot to foot.

"With you there I know I can do it."

"Do what?"

"The buckle," Luke said. "Win the buckle!"

19

The Kamloops rodeo grounds were larger than any other on the circuit. The stands held several thousand fans. And they were crowded now. It was the last day of the provincials. The championship rounds were being held.

And Luke was in them. As one of the top 10 cowboys for the season, he had qualified for the finals. And he had ridden well on his first ride.

He had drawn a big Simmental. It had gone into a spin, but Luke had pulled it out. The clown had gotten the bull's attention. Luke straightened out and kept the bull moving across the arena. At the horn he was still firm on the bull. He had yanked his hand loose from the rigging and slid to the soft dirt.

Then he waited. He heard a cheer go up and looked at the points board. An 88. Good enough for second. He was going in just two points behind the leader, Les Martin.

He and Bel had a celebration dinner. They had cooked steaks on their Coleman stove. And they had drunk a bottle of red wine. It even had a cork in it.

Then Luke had tried to study. But it was too hard. He put his books down and got out of the camper. He had begun to pace. Bel came out and sat on the picnic table.

"You're pretty wound up, Luke," she said. "Is it me? Do I make you nervous?"

Luke turned to her and shook his head.

"No, no. It's not that. It's the $5,000. The championship. It's just that so much is riding on tomorrow's bull."

Bel smiled. "That's right. So much is. You."

Luke laughed nervously.

"No, I mean it," Bel went on. "Win or lose, you're what counts. Not the buckle. Not the money."

Luke had nodded. But he didn't sleep much.

That was yesterday. Now Luke and Bel were walking toward the announcement board. Luke was waiting to see what bull he had drawn. The trophy case was on one side. He pulled Bel over to it.

"There," he exclaimed, pointing to the bull riding buckle. "There it is." The gold stitching around the silver gleamed in the bright sun. The six garnets glowed blood red.

"It's very pretty," Bel said.

"Pretty?" Luke shook his head. "Bel, it's more than pretty. It's beautiful. It's everything I've worked for."

"Everything? What about us, Luke?"

"No, no," Luke waved his hands back and forth. "I don't mean that. It's just that… That maybe I'll finally be someone."

Bel looked sad. She patted Luke gently on the cheek.

Suddenly cowboys started rushing over to the announcement

board. The mounts had been posted. Luke walked quickly to the board. He found the sheet for the bull riders. His name was second. He was riding bull Number 19. He looked at the list of bulls posted next to the sheet. A chill ran down his back.

Bull 19 was Sundial.

"Well, you haven't missed much as far as Sundial goes," Harvey said. They were walking toward the chutes for Luke's ride. "In the three years you've been gone he's only been ridden once."

"Then he is rideable," Luke said.

"Just barely. And be careful with him. He seems to be getting ornerier in his old age. He almost killed Sandy Jordan over at Salmon Arm. He threw him and then danced all over him."

The two men neared the chutes.

"Guess I won't need you on flank strap this time, partner," Luke said. The championships had professionals handling the flank straps. "I'll miss you."

"I'll be on the boards. With Bel. We'll be there with you." He stuck out his hand. "Good luck, Luke."

Luke took his hand and shook it. Then he turned and climbed over the chute boards.

Sundial looked as big and mean as Luke remembered him. The big Brahman paced nervously inside the chute. He snorted and swung his massive head from side to side.

Luke pulled the leather glove onto his right hand. Then he lowered himself onto the broad back of the bull. He sat just behind the Brahman's hump. The chute man handed Luke the rigging. And Luke began to wrap it around his hand.

He brought the leather rope across his palm. Then he wrapped it around the back of his hand and back across his palm. He sat for a moment staring at the rope in his hand. Then he looped it around his thumb and yanked it firm. He pulled his hand into the trembling flesh of the bull.

If there was ever a ride where he needed a suicide wrap, this was it.

He pulled the rigging tight. His right arm was taut. His spurs were positioned over the bull's shoulders. He felt the adrenaline pump through him. The bell clanged underneath as the bull shuddered nervously. Luke nodded at the gate man.

"Chute!" he yelled.

Luke kept his head up as Sundial burst from the chutes. His eyes were riveted on the bull's shoulders. Luke was ready for him to dive right like the last time. But the bull kept charging straight out into the arena.

Everything was quiet. Luke couldn't hear the bell. The crowd was a silent blur. He was focussed on the ride. Sundial pulled left, but Luke straightened him. The seconds ticked away.

The bull yanked right, throwing Luke's head violently to the side. But Luke recovered. He held on like he was stuck to the bull's back. He heaved and jerked as the bull desperately plunged and bucked. A few more seconds ticked away. Even in the silence Luke knew he had it. Just one or two more seconds.

Then Luke wasn't sure what happened. The bull had been

charging straight across the arena. He had built up speed. Suddenly Luke felt the bull's legs plant in the soft dirt. Luke was sure he was going into a dive. He braced himself. But then Luke almost ripped in two. He felt himself and the bull rise straight up. He thought they were headed for the bright sun overhead. He sensed that all four of the bull's legs were off the ground. Luke was doubled over Sundial's back.

And then they hit. There was pain. Confusion. He heard the horn. His feet were on the ground. He was being dragged by his thumb still lashed into the rigging. The pain screamed down his arm.

Sundial charged at the boards. Luke was across the bull's right side. His right hand was still tied to the bull's back. At the last minute the big bull swung. Luke was smashed against the boards. He felt a sharp pain in his chest. Then the bull dragged him along the side of the arena. He felt his face collide with a post. He was almost unconscious. Luke heard people screaming and jerking backwards as the bull rushed by. Now he was being yanked back toward the centre of the arena. He had to untie his thumb.

The bull was kicking and bucking. Luke managed to swing his left hand up onto the bull's back. He grabbed at the rigging still tied around his thumb. He felt dampness. He tore at the leather rope. The bull kept bucking. He tore at it again. Finally it released. With one last twist the bull threw him in the air. His rear hoof caught Luke on the side of his head. Luke fell to the dirt and passed out.

20

"But did I ride it?" Luke asked again. "Did I ride it?"

"Please settle down, Mr. Tronson."

Luke looked up. A nurse in a white dress and hat was looking at a bottle next to him. He began to lapse back into unconsciousness.

"Please," he pleaded. "Tell me. Did I ride the bull?"

The nurse shook her head in exasperation. Then she smiled sweetly. She patted him on his good arm. "Mr. Tronson, you've got 50 stitches in your thumb. And that's just outside. You've got a smashed cheek bone. Three broken ribs. Your eyelid is split wide open. You almost lost your eye! I don't think we should be worrying about any old bull."

"Did I ride it?" he mumbled. The darkness was giving way again. He was aware of a shooting pain in his right arm. It hurt to breathe. He seemed to be able to see only out of one eye.

Harvey's face swam into view.

Luke tried to sit up. The pain was too great. He lay back down.

"For God's sake, Harvey. Tell me. Did I ride him?"

Harvey's face was grim. He ran his fingers through his black hair.

"Jesus, Luke," he said. "You almost died out there."

Luke tried to scream at him, but all he could manage was a gasp. "For God's sake, Harvey, I've got to know. Did I ride him?"

There was a long pause. "Well, little buddy," Harvey said softly, "it was close. Your feet hit the ground just as the horn went."

Luke sank back into the sheets.

"But they gave it to you."

Now Luke did sit up. He looked directly into Harvey's grinning face.

"You son of a bitch, Harvey. Why didn't you tell me?" he rasped.

Harvey laughed. "The nurse told me not to get you too excited. Oh, and Luke, they gave you something else."

Harvey took out a black leather box. It was about 12 inches long. He handed it to Luke. Luke took the box in his left hand and lifted the hinged lid. The buckle rested on a bed of red velvet. "Luke Tronson" had been engraved on the scroll underneath the gold bull. Luke lay back on the bed. He closed his one eye. Tears squeezed out the edges.

"Luke, I never want to watch you ride again." Bel sat on the side of his bed. Her eyes were red.

"But honey, it's not always like this," Luke said.

"I don't care!" Bel cried. "I never want to see that again. I was dying with you out there. I was screaming and screaming!"

Luke reached over with his left hand and squeezed her knee.

"I'm sorry. I wanted this so much. I wanted it for you."

"Don't give me that crap anymore, Luke Tronson," Bel sobbed. "You wanted it for *you*! And you almost killed yourself getting it! What about me? And the baby?"

"What baby? We don't have a baby."

"Well, we're going to."

"We are?"

"We are."

Luke stared at Bel. He wished he had two good eyes.

"But I don't know if I'll be any good. As a parent. Maybe I'll be like my dad!"

"You won't be," Bel said confidently.

"How do you know?"

" 'Cause you're not your dad. And anyway, I won't let you be."

Luke lay still and quiet for a long time. Then he reached over on the table beside his bed. He picked up the leather box.

"Here. It's for you."

Bel opened the box. She stared at the gold and silver buckle inside. Its red garnets seemed to soak up the red of the velvet. She traced Luke's name with her finger.

"I, I can't, Luke. It's yours. It's what you always wanted," Bel whispered.

Luke was quiet for a long moment.

"Nah, not really," he said at last.

The thumb throbbed on his right hand. He had a splitting headache. But he felt good. Better than he had in years.